Edited by: Partners In Crime Book Services

Cover design and formatting by: Rebecca Poole of Dreams2media

SPIDER'S RETURN

TL SHIVELY

Acknowledgements

I just want to say thank you to everyone for reading these stories and wanting more. You are what makes writing these stories so worthwhile.

I would like to send a heavenly happy birthday to my father-in-law, Norwood Bush Jr. If he were here today, I know he would be one of my biggest supporters. He is greatly missed by his family.

Love you, Dad.

CHAPTER 1

The sounds of battle filled the air around her as Calista barely dodged energy blasts. They were so close she could feel the heat radiating from each one. No greenery filled the landscape around her, only a barren and unforgiving terrain that seemed to stretch out forever. A terrain she couldn't place, and she was sure she had seen them all in her many years.

"I need to rethink having you as a best friend."

Calista jerked around to see a male winking at her, his dark eyes twinkling beneath his long, dark locks that hung down around his tattooed face. A male she had never seen before but was looking at her as if they were good friends.

"C'mon Kaine, where's your sense of adventure?" The amused voice of Solen froze Calista where she stood. Her whole body felt numb as she slowly turned to see Solen smiling at her, that roguish smile she saw so much in her dreams. "You okay, Spider?" His smile slipped slightly as his brow furrowed with concern.

Kaine slammed into Solen as a bright bolt of pure white flew past them, hitting the boulder where Solen had stood only moments before. The boulder exploded into dust particles that showered down on them upon impact.

"I can't always be around to save your ass," Kaine grunted as he kneeled down, placing his hand on the ground, staring past Calista with an intense gaze. "These interlopers really need to be evicted." Looking down, Calista saw his hands glowing brightly while arcs of pure energy raced along the surface of the ground towards the silver ancients that were advancing towards them.

Ancients? They were back?

"Spider! Watch out!" Solen grabbed her, twirling them both around so she was pressed against a boulder with him smiling down at her. She could hear the impact of an energy bolt that was meant for her demolishing the area they once stood in. "That was close." She looked up into his eyes, feeling her heart tighten at his loving gaze, right before a flash of light lit up all around them. As she watched his eyes went wide with the shock of what was happening, he opened his mouth as if to say something and then went slack in her arms.

"Noooooo!" The scream pulled from her was so gut wrenching that when she jerked up in her bed, she felt as if she had no breath left in her lungs. Looking around the room, she realized that she was still in her small apartment in Georgia. No battles with the Ancients, no heroic Solen dying in her arms and no dark-haired stranger with glowing hands. "Pull it together, Calista." She attempted to calm her pounding heart and shaky nerves but no matter what pep talk she gave herself, her hands still shook.

Rising from the bed, she moved to the bathroom where she saw her pale face staring back at her from the mirror. "Guess I won't be getting any more sleep tonight." Glancing at the clock that shone from the top of her dresser, she saw it was after five in the morning. She could use a drink but she knew that there was no club open in Georgia at that time, at least not any she knew of. But she knew of one city that never slept. With a thought, her night clothes morphed into a black jumpsuit with matching high heels and clutch bag. "Sin City, here I come," she said as she shimmered out of sight.

Within moments, Calista was standing next to the road on the main strip in Las Vegas. Even though it was two in the morning in Vegas, the strip was so lit up you couldn't even tell how late it was. People were milling around as if it was eight in the evening, although there were some that you wouldn't see out at that time of day. Their time was the night. Calista ignored them all as she headed towards her destination: the hidden speakeasy that very few knew of. One small push on a certain bookcase and she walked into her favorite bar in Vegas.

Tonight, she wasn't in the mood for the colored

strobe lights, loud music, nor the stale smells of a packed nightclub. She just wanted a drink and maybe a dance or two. She moved past those seated at the padded couches and chairs set up for a relaxed discussion of their choice. At the bar stood a man dressed in perfect 1920s bartender attire all the way down to the black arm garters over his white sleeves.

The man gave a gentlemanly nod as she reached the bar, a genuine smile on his face as he twisted a white cloth inside the lowball glass that he was polishing. "And what would the lady desire this night?"

Leaning against the bar, she looked out over the speakeasy at everyone to see if she could get an idea of what she would like to drink. Unfortunately, nothing seemed to pop out at her. Looking back at the bartender, her lips twisted slightly. "Not sure what I want." Her head tilted as she looked at him. "What do you suggest?"

He leaned back, still rubbing the glass with that white rag, watching her as if sizing her up. "What can you handle?"

The laughter that erupted from Calista at his question had his brows raising. She held up a perfectly manicured hand before he got offended at her response. "I'm sorry, no offense, but I can promise you there is nothing that I can't handle."

He placed the glass that he had in his hand, one that she was sure was cleaner than Rowena's temple back in Atlantis. "In that case, how about a John Stahle?"

Calista's brow furrowed. "A John Stahle? What is that?"

Pouring some amber liquid into the lowball glass with ice, he smirked. "A drink I made up, so I named it after myself." He shrugged his shoulders, the smirk still in place, as he pulled out the soda gun. Pushing a button, more amber liquid filled the glass.

"A bit conceited, don't you think?" Calista looked back up into his face.

He pushed the drink towards her on the bar. "Try it out and decide for yourself, sweetheart."

Calista looked from him to the drink before lifting up the glass, throwing some bills on the bar. "I will." She grinned, turning sharply on her heel and walked away, lifting the glass to her lips. She tasted bourbon and ginger, not a combination she ever had before. Not a bad drink but no way would she tell the bartender that, his head was big enough as is.

There was a makeshift small dance floor where some wore 1920's attire, while most wore outfits you would see out on the strip. Calista weaved through the ones dancing on the floor, letting the music flow through her and move her body to the beat. She felt the slender body moving behind her, matching her moves. Turning with her drink still in hand she felt her heart contract, there looking down at her with a lopsided grin was Solen. She let him wrap his arms around her as they danced to the music. She wanted to ask how it was that he was here

5

but felt it would ruin the moment. So, she stayed quiet as they danced.

"What do you think you are doing?"

Calista was jerked away from the dance floor and her dancing partner by an angry looking brunette. She turned back to see the man she had been dancing with and felt her stomach clench. Gone was Solen's roguish grin, instead stood a guy with clean-shaven, neatly spiked hair that was so greased down with gel, she couldn't accurately determine the color.

Looking around the room, she realized they had become the main attraction. Something that she had always stayed away from, getting attraction in this day and age always ended up on social media. That would guarantee a visit from the dragon brothers, which isn't bad when it's just Rikar but when Draken joins his brother, she knows she's in for a full session of overprotective brothering 101.

When she went to remove herself from the situation, the angry woman grabbed at her again, jerking her around. "Where do you think you're going?" The woman's belligerent voice and attitude was a full-frontal assault.

Calista refused to rise to the bait. She stared at the woman, letting her power show very minutely in her eyes, enough to give them a low glow. "You don't want to do this, trust me." The woman may have been belligerent but at least she had the smarts to back down and let Calista walk away with her empty glass, whose contents had been thrown on the now silent dance floor.

As she walked through the crowds, she kept seeing Solen's face grinning at her, looking concerned and then the worst one of all. The one with the lifeless eyes and slack jawed mouth. Her chest tightened with each step, almost stumbling each time she saw his face. She knew this wasn't right, that this wasn't real, but it didn't stop the feelings of dread that made her blood go cold.

"Cali?"

On one of the padded chairs sat her younger brother Eon, looking up at her with concern. "What are you doing here, Eon?" she asked him, then realizing how quiet it had become, she looked around them. Everyone seemed to be frozen in time, her brother's specialty. Something he shares with their grandfather the Atlantean God, Tylaos. Not only is he the ruler of the Atlantean pantheon, but he is also the god of time and technology. "Why did you have to freeze everyone?"

"Because mortals have hang-ups about the young being in such an establishment," he told her simply, sitting in that chair with his feet barely reaching the floor. You wouldn't guess that he was several centuries old just by looking at him.

"Wouldn't take you much to make yourself older, you know?" She crossed her arms looking down at her brother with sisterly love. Growing up in Greece with Ares and the others gave her a greater appreciation for

7

the loving family dynamic she had in Atlantis. Her and Eon were close, he was the one God from Atlantis who never needed a reason to come visit his big sister. He was also the one they sent when they needed her home.

Eon lifted a dismissive shoulder. "I prefer this form. I have no desire for the messiness that comes with age." Calista raised a brow but he just gave her one of his boyish grins that always pulled at her heart, the brow lowered and her lips curved into a smile she reserved only for him. "With age comes expectations, you know that. I hate expectations." He gave an arrogant nod that reminded her of Draken, who happened to be Eon's idol, unfortunately. Which meant that he would give Draken updates any time he asked, although Calista was still able to convince her brother to keep some things between them.

"You could've gone invisible," she countered back. During the time of the curse, there were no new births, but since the curse was lifted, there had been several. One of them had dropped his superior demeanor to roll his eyes at her.

"And you're wasting time." He hopped down off of his chair and looked up at her. "Mom and Pops sent me to fetch you; you're needed back home."

She couldn't suppress the sigh that escaped. "I don't suppose you're going to tell me the reason?"

"I'm just a kid." He grabbed her hand, looking up at her. "I do what I'm told."

"Since when?" Calista snorted as he pulled them both into a whirling vortex of blue and black.

CHAPTER 2

When the world finally righted itself, Calista frowned down at her unrepentant brother. "Why can't you shimmer like the rest of us? You know I hate it when you use your vortexes to travel."

Eon just shrugged as he started down one of the neatly cobbled roads of Atlantis. "Shimmering is dull and boring."

"Can't have that." Eon grinned at the sarcasm in her voice; not much rattled him. While Calista was mostly like their father, in attitude and actions mostly, Eon had their mother's characteristics. Both Eon and their mother were the calm to the tumultuous Calista and Cael.

"Goddess Calista."

Calista looked to her right, pausing and smiling as Syles, one of her acolytes, came rushing up to greet her. She had to admit, even after all these years of being the Goddess of Manipulation and having her own temple with worshippers, it was hard to get used to being worshiped. Syles stopped in front of her and gave a graceful bow, lowering only slightly at the waist, in greeting.

"Hello Syles, how are you doing?" Calista smiled at the red-haired beauty.

"I'm doing well, goddess," Syles responded.

"Syles, how many times have we been over this? *Calista*. How many times must I tell you that you don't have to call me goddess?" Calista shook her head in wonder.

"As always, at least one more." Syles gave a cheeky grin that had Calista laughing. "Your temple has been prepared for your arrival; your parents let us know Eon was on his way to fetch you. You have plenty of fruit and nectar but if there is anything else that you desire, I will do my due diligence to make it happen."

No matter that she mostly lived in the world above, only coming home for brief moments to visit throughout the years, it never ceased to amaze her that her worshippers would greet her appearance with the same reverence they did the rest of the Atlanteans. "Thank you, Syles, I'm sure everything is perfect." With that, Syles gave another graceful bow and moved on with her duties.

"They miss you; you know?"

"I miss them too, Eon. I miss all of you, but I've made myself a life up there with the mortals," Calista replied watching Syles walking away, stopping every so often to speak to another along her way. "I can't just walk away from all that."

"Oh no, can't walk away from a place where you have to pretend to grow old, fake your own death every four or five decades and then start all over again somewhere new." The sarcasm dripping from Eon's words told her that she did have some influence over him. Probably not the best. And his sarcasm wasn't done yet. "Why would you want to live where you don't have to worry about pretending to be something you aren't, where people accept you for who you are?" He shook his head and started back down the path towards their parents' temple.

Her lips twisted as she watched him stalking away. Why did that feel like a chat with Draken? Maybe she should think about staying home more; Eon seemed to be spending too much time with the dragon brothers. As if he could read her mind, he stopped and turned to look at her. "Are you going to just stand there or follow?" She raised a brow at him; yeah, definitely too much time with the dragons.

"Let's go see what Mom and Dad want." Calista started down the path after him, doing her best to bite her tongue and not call him a mini-Draken. Although he would probably take that as a compliment.

To this day she still loved walking into her mother's temple. Even with her mother being the goddess of war, strategy, and planning, her temple still had a welcoming air. Flowers were all over as well as colored accents that adorned the walls. Her and Eon walked through the hallways, past their mother's war room as well as her planning rooms until they reached the back of the temple. There was the door to the temple that their parents shared, a combination of them both. The elegant beauty of their mother and the bedlam that was their father, somehow, together, they made it work.

Pictures of all sorts hung on the walls as well as sculptures of the people of Atlantis that was done by either Atmos or one of his followers. Then the ones of Calista, Eon and other family members that had their own special places in the alcoves high up on the walls.

"Are you seriously going to act like a tourist?"

Calista turned to look at her brother who was giving her a condescending look. "How am I acting like a tourist?" she countered, to which he rolled his eyes, turning away from her and walking through the archway to their parents' personal domicile in their temple. Giving her head a slow shake, she followed.

"Cali!" As soon as she entered the room, her mother embraced her. "It's been too long." After kissing Calista's cheek, her mother moved back, allowing her father to lift Calista into his arms.

"There's my girl!" His voice boomed as he looked down on his daughter with twinkling eyes.

"Hey, Dad." Calista leaned her head against his chest, loving the feeling of being in her dad's arms for the moment. "I've missed you both."

"There is a way to remedy that." Her mother smiled as she led Calista to the cushioned lounges, watching as Cael and Eon clapped hands together before joining them. As they sat down, Cael ruffled Eon's hair, laughing when Eon threw him dark looks. Eon hated having his hair messed up, although Calista had a feeling that, deep down, he liked when their father messed with him like that.

Calista grabbed some berries from one of the bowls on the center table in the room before turning to look at her mother. "So, why was I summoned home?"

"Can't we want some time with our daughter?" Her father asked.

She sighed. "Of course you can, but if that was the case, I don't think Eon would've showed up in the middle of the night."

Cael grinned proudly. "My daughter's so smart."

"Our daughter," Malis corrected him.

"Of course, my love," Cael agreed but as soon as Malis looked away he mouthed MINE to Calista, who barely held back her laughter. She really did miss her parents.

"We can discuss why you were needed here later." Her mother smiled at her. "I'm sure you want to spend some time with your acolytes."

Averting her gaze, Calista bit her lip.

"Calista? What is it?" She could hear the concern in her mother's voice but wasn't sure how to put her feelings into words. Malis turned towards Cael and Eon who had fallen onto the floor from wrestling around. "Why don't you go let Rikar and Draken know Calista is home?"

"Yeah!" Eon jumped up with bright eyes before twirling around and leaping through the blue and black vortex he just created.

"You don't need to vortex everywhere!" Malis attempted to grab Eon but the vortex closed on itself as soon as he entered. Malis shot Cael an exasperated look, to which he just grinned. "Cael!"

"I'll go get him." Cael laughed, shimmering out of sight.

Malis sighed, turning to Calista. "Not much has changed with those two." Settling back against the lounge arm she asked, "So, what is wrong, my daughter?"

Calista looked down at the pendant hanging from her necklace, Scratch encased in the tear drop crystal. How she missed him, her fingers reaching for the pendant, holding it gently between them as she often did when troubled.

"Cali?"

"I'm still not comfortable having acolytes, Mom," she finally confessed. "I know." She grimaced at the look in her mother's eyes.

"Cali, you've had your temple for many millennia now. Why have you never told me this?"

Calista groaned and burrowed deeper into the cushions behind her, wishing she had left with her father and brother. "I didn't want to say anything, didn't want you and Dad to be disappointed in me."

"Calista!" She looked up at the gentle censor she heard in her mother's voice. "There is nothing you could do that would change the way your father and I think of you. Besides," her mother's voice carried amusement. "You're not the only deity to have issues such as this."

"I'm not?"

"No." Her mother moved closer, placing her hand on top of Calista's gently. That simple touch brought a smile to Calista's face, filling her with more confidence and acceptance. "It took your father quite a while to get used to his temple and acolytes."

Calista's mouth fell open hearing that; her father had always seemed so confident and self-assured. She couldn't imagine him floundering like she had been. "How did he eventually get used to it?"

"Not sure if I ever truly got used to it." Her father walked into the room grinning at her, his eyes full of pride. "But I listened to your mother when she told me to stop thinking that the acolytes were there to serve me." Calista frowned, unsure of what he meant. He knelt in front of her, grasping both their hands in his. "I realized I'm there to help them. We work alongside our acolytes; we don't rule them."

"Does everyone feel that way here?" She had to admit none of the acolytes seemed to fear any of the Gods or Goddesses here.

"In one way or another." Her mother smiled; leaning forward, she kissed Calista's brow. "Now, go see how you can help your acolytes before Rikar and Draken find you."

"Yes, Mom." Calista grinned broadly feeling more

confident, then paused before shimmering out. "If they were the ones who wanted to see me, why couldn't they come themselves?"

"They said something about you always seeming to disappear whenever they came shoreside," her mother informed her.

"I wonder why," she muttered.

Her father laughed. "Give them a chance. They only want to protect you."

"They call it protecting, I call it smothering," she countered. "Draken is mated, why doesn't he stick to smothering his mate and leave me be?"

Malis laughed, "He doesn't get away with that when it comes to her."

Calista snorted. "I think I need to get together with Kimi so she can give me some tips."

"Might want to wait a bit on that." Cael winked at his daughter, who was looking curiously at him.

"Cael," her mother reprimanded him. "That is Draken's news to tell."

"You're right, my love." Cale grinned down at Malis, leaning to kiss her gently on her lips.

"On that note." Calista stood up. "I'm outta here." She shimmered out but not before she heard her father laugh and say, "That's one way to clear a room."

"This better not be one of Draken's or Rikar's

tricks," Calista muttered as she shimmered into the entry of her temple. "If it is, Dad will get those dragon rugs he keeps threatening them with." Taking a deep breath, she walked through the halls of her temple, smiling as she saw the pictures and statues of her family all around her. Atmos and his acolytes made sure to keep her pictures up to date, even when she wasn't around.

The sound of scurrying legs across the marble floor was the only warning she had before Blue leapt onto her arms that were folded in front of her. "Blue!" She smiled and kissed the head of her little friend, who was already nuzzling the teardrop crystal. "I know, I miss him too." Blue settled into the crook of her arm as she moved further into her temple. Through the years she had made friends with many other eight-legged critters but they all knew that her shoulder was off limits, that was Scratch's spot.

There were several lounge chairs throughout the temple, black cushions with splashes of colored blankets draped across them. Tables with bowls of fruit that were placed by her acolytes, although she was sure Salis also had a hand in it, upon seeing a wheat stem laying casually on top of one of the bowls. As the Atlantean God of Agriculture and Inspiration, it was one of his symbols. Growing up in Greece, she never had a place to call her own, only whatever hiding places she could find throughout the land. Closing her eyes with a sigh, she silently berated herself; sometimes it still felt like she never left that land and those who did their best to belittle and demean her. She was a goddess who had a title and a temple, why did she still think about her time in Greece?

"Hello, Goddess Calista."

Turning around she smiled at Syles. "Hello, I'm sorry I haven't been around."

But Syles was shaking her head. "You have no reason to apologize, Goddess. We're happy to have you home."

"We?"

"Your other acolytes, they didn't want to impose on you, so they have stayed their distance," Syles explained, although Calista wasn't sure how she felt about them feeling as if they couldn't approach her. "Please don't fret, Goddess. They want you to be comfortable." It didn't do much to appease her uneasiness but Calista nodded. "Is there anything that I can do for you?"

Calista breathed in, about to tell Syles that she was good, but instead she said, "How about giving me a heads up before the brothers show up?"

Syles laughed, which in turn made Calista smile, feeling not so distant. "I can do that, Goddess."

"Our relationship is well known, huh?" Calista said ruefully.

Syles gave a semi-shrug. "The brothers' reputation with the ladies and their over protectiveness with you are very well known. No worries, I'm used to their charm. Besides, I'm your acolyte, not theirs."

Calista gave her a thankful smile as Syles moved from the room, a purple spider scurrying after her. That was a nice sight to see. Calista had never picked a head acolyte for her temple, she had never been home long enough to even consider it, but she was thinking that was truly a disservice to Syles. Maybe after she found out what the brothers wanted, she would have to make some adjustments.

CHAPTER 3

Moving past the open sitting area, Calista entered her own private sanctum, letting the heavy drapes fall behind her. Stairs off to her right led up to a window seat adorned with cushions of all colors, in front of a large circular window that looked out upon all of Atlantis. She had spent many nights on those cushions, just staring out over her beautiful home before falling asleep. Over on one of her desks sat some trinkets from her time above in the mortal world and down here below in Atlantis. Her eyes widened when she saw something that wasn't supposed to be here. The wooden Atlantean alphabet bridge that she knew belonged in the caves of the brothers. Moving closer, she lifted one of the alphabet blocks, curious how it came to be here. It was her favorite piece from the caves but she had never deigned to remove it.

Replacing the block back in its place, she looked around her sanctum. There were scrolls, codexes and books on tables, in shelves, and on the nightstand by her bed. Growing up with Ares, she had never been allowed to further herself intellectually. Since coming to

Atlantis, her love of reading had grown. During the years since Solen left, she read much about the stars but never found the answer she had been looking for. How to find Solen. It had been so long; she didn't even know if he was still alive. She was a goddess, after all; that was why she was still alive. What if his people were like the mortals that walked the land above? Life so fleeting that it was gone with a blink of an immortal eye. On one of her bookshelves, in a frame next to the rolled scroll that told the story of the great battle of Atlantis, was a painted picture of Draken, Rikar, Solen and herself. There on her shoulder was scratch in his favorite perch.

She released a sigh, still staring at the picture, back when they were happy and fun-loving. Draken was always the most serious between him and Rikar, but he still knew how to have fun. She had to admit that several times it was at her expense but something she wouldn't mind today if it brought back the old Draken. She missed him. When he found out about her phoenix tattoo that adorned her right side, from her ribs down to below her hips, he picked on her about jumping in head-first instead of dipping her toes in. Of course, hers is nothing compared to the brothers with their dragon tattoos that covered their backs.

Moving up the stairs to the window, she knelt down on the cushions looking out over Atlantis, into the watery depths that were being held back by Rowena's protection veil. Somewhere out there in the depths was

Poseidon's temple, where Draken and Rikar had been summoned all those centuries ago. No one knows what happened during that time, they had been gone for almost a full century but when they returned home to Atlantis, nothing was the same. Gone was the fun-loving Draken who teased her and made her smile even when she wanted to slap him, in his place was someone she barely recognized. He was still overprotective of her, possibly even more so but they were no longer as close as they used to be. Even her father remarked on how distant Draken had become.

Rikar was still the same fun-loving, flirtatious, easygoing lover boy he always was. Something that had puzzled her and others, what happened that changed Draken so much but yet Rikar stayed the same? No one knew what happened and both brothers are tight-lipped about their time with their father.

Everyone was amazed when he found his wife, Kimi. She was gentle and caring, they had hoped she would be able to change him, bring him back to his former self. Hadn't happened yet, although she had to be honest that it wasn't like she saw him in his home with Kimi. Maybe he was different there. She only met Kimi briefly, but after her mother saying how Kimi never let him get away with his overbearingness with her, she was beginning to rethink that. It might be nice to see someone tell Draken no and see it stick. Her lips curled into a grin as she imagined Draken's hard expression turning into a pout when he couldn't get his way. Yes, a visit to Kimi was definitely on the agenda now.

A movement down on one of the cobbled streets caught her attention, Brax and his daughter Shaylane were walking together, smiling and laughing. When Calista first met Brax, he had no personality, unless you count being a jerk. She couldn't remember him ever smiling, only stating facts with barely any emotion. Now you have Draken being the stick in the mud and Brax was enjoying life. She had asked Vesper, the God of Chaos and Mayhem, if he had a hand in it but even his sister claimed he was innocent.

"Geronimo!" The sound of her brother running into her sanctum echoed all around the room. Calista turned in time to see him launch himself from the lower floor to her bed that was positioned on top of a platform. Grabbing an errant scroll that had gone flying when he landed, he started to unroll it and read. "Draken will see you now," he told her without looking up from the scroll. Calista opened her mouth to tell him that she doesn't answer to either of the brothers but closed it on a sigh. Not like Eon would pay her any mind any ways.

"Goddess Calista." Syles entered the Sanctum cautiously, looking around.

Calista smiled. "The brothers are here?"

Syles nodded. "Do you want me to have them wait for you in the sitting area?"

Calista shook her head. "We both know they wouldn't and I would never put you in such a situation."

Syles nodded in gratitude, moving out to let the brothers know she would be coming out momentarily. She was walking out of her room when she heard Draken growling, "Since when do we need to be announced for Calista?"

"When it comes to the two of you, I need a heads up," Calista told him without flinching.

Rikar grinned, moving swiftly to her and lifting her up in one of his giant hugs that always left her breathless. Kissing her head, he grinned down at her. "Have missed you, princess." He told her with his eyes twinkling with mirth.

Then there was Draken, who was staring at her with hooded eyes, his mouth set in a hard line, as normal. Breathing in, she moved over to him, placing a hand on his shoulder, she used him for support to lean up and kiss his cheek. "Hello, Draken." She smiled up at him but still no softening. Looking around she frowned up at him. "Where is Kimi?"

"She's home," was the curt answer, an answer that had her putting her hands on her hips leveling him with a hard stare. He sighed before answering her, "she's home taking care of our son."

Calista's eyes widened, as her mouth dropped open hearing him say that.

"Careful, princess, you're going to catch flies and deprive Blue of her dinner." Rikar smirked at her but she paid him no mind as she jumped up to hug Draken.

"That is awesome! I'm so happy for you!" she told him, feeling his arms move awkwardly to hug her back. Still beaming, she laughed. "So, when do I get to meet my nephew?"

"If you didn't avoid us when we would come shoreside, you would've already," he replied in that condescending manner of his that he used when he was unhappy with her.

"If I had known you were a father and wanted to introduce me to my new nephew, I wouldn't have tried to avoid you," she told him smartly. His darkening expression told her that he didn't find the humor in her words. Although, Rikar was barely holding his laughter back. Rikar had the calm, fun loving nature that would temper Draken's hard and unbending ways, but when it came down to it, he would back up his brother completely. That was very well known. "So, when do I get to see Draken Jr?" she asked again.

"That's not his name." Draken growled at her.

"I'm too old for this crud." Rikar spoke in a Romanian accent, catching Calista's attention.

"I know that show." She got excited. "*The Last Bite*. I watch it every Thursday night. That character is so dreamy."

"No encouraging him," Draken told her with a frown. "Bad enough, I have him spouting off lines from that stupid show."

"Have you ever watched it?" she countered.

"No, and I'm not going to." Draken crossed his arms, showing her that he considered that the end of the discussion.

"Well, you're missing out," she told him haughtily, enjoying the narrowing of his eyes.

"I think we need a date night with *The Last Bite,* popcorn and Chocolate Buttons." Rikar winked at her, pulling her attention from his brother. She forgot she had told him of her fondness for the mortal treat, Chocolate Buttons.

"Maybe we do." Turning from Rikar, she looked at Draken. "We could always have it at your place with Kimi and my nephew, whose name you haven't told me."

Another growl was aimed her way before Draken finally told her, "Calton."

"Nice strong name." Calista gave a sharp nod. "So, next Thursday, your place. You, Rikar, Kimi, Calton and me."

"And me!" They laughed hearing Eon shouting from the other room.

Draken crossed his arms, staring at her thoughtfully. "You show up, I will make sure to be there with your favorite treats."

"I'm holding you to that!" Calista pushed her forefinger against his chest, but he gave no reaction other than a slight brow raise. "Eeek!" She shrieked as Rikar wrapped his arms around her waist, pulling her away from Draken.

"Enough of that before you end up on your ass, princess. You know you can only push him so much." Rikar grinned at her as he sat her down on one of her padded lounges. She stuck her tongue out at him but he just laughed. "Very mature, princess." That prompted a not so nice gesture that had him laughing and Draken giving her a barely tolerable look.

Leaning back against the cushions, she crossed her arms staring at them both. "So, was that why my brother came to get me in the middle of the night? To tell me that I'm an aunt?"

"Not exactly," Rikar drawled slowly.

Calista rose and raised a brow at him, leveling him with a stern stare that had about as much impact as any of the others. "So, exactly why was I summoned then?"

"That would be me."

That voice!

Calista froze.

Draken growled.

Rikar's eyes narrowed on her.

Turning slowly around, there standing in the doorway to the entrance to her temple, was one of the two men from the nightmare that sent her to the nightclub. "Kaine?"

Kaine's eyes widened upon hearing her call him by name but before anything else could be said Draken half-shifted into his dragon form and had Kaine pressed against the wall, with his teeth bared.

CHAPTER 4

"Draken! NO!" Calista shouted moving to pull him off of Kaine, except that Rikar pulled her back before she could. "What are you doing?" She turned frowning at Rikar. "Let me go!" She wiggled erratically in his arms.

"Stay still, princess." Rikar attempted to calm her but she was having none of that.

"No, Draken needs to back down," she told him, still struggling, attempting to shimmer out of his arms. When she failed to do so, Rikar using his power to keep her pinned, she slammed her high heeled boot on the inside of his foot. Granting her a momentarily reprieve, she shimmered next to Draken and Kaine, placing her hand on Draken's scaled arm. "Enough, Draken! Let Kaine go." She shouted in an attempt to break through to him.

"You know him?" Draken's voice was more dragon than man, his eyes slitted although his gaze never left Kaine's, whose expression went from very tight-lipped to rapid blinking at her.

"You do?" Kaine asked her.

She could feel the hard stare of Rikar on her back and knew she needed to diffuse this situation quickly. The brother's powers were great but she knew from her dream that Kaine wasn't without his own power. She didn't need these three battling, there could be much damage to Atlantis if they weren't subdued. "He is Solen's best friend."

Those words stopped both of them as Draken's eyes went back to human although his hands still held their claw-like appearance. He looked at her with a frown. "Solen's best friend? Thought that was Rikar and I."

That moment was all Kaine needed to shove Draken back and move out of his way so that he couldn't put him back up against the wall. "Sorry to disappoint you, lizard boy," Kaine sneered at him. "But I've known Solen since childhood."

Draken moved closer to him but Calista moved in between them, placing one hand on Draken's chest. "Enough!" Draken glared down at her with a growl but she stood her ground, her jaw tightened as she stared back at him, refusing to back down.

"We don't even know what he wants," Draken growled.

"Well, you weren't going to find that out with your arm against his throat," she told him, her eyes flashing with her aggravation. "You weren't even giving him a chance to tell you why he was here."

"You're defending him?" Draken looked taken aback by her defiance. "Over your family?"

"Draken..." She moved closer to him, her hands reaching out in a coaxing manner but it was too late. His eyes practically shuttered to her as he left in a whirl-wind of water that blew papers, cushions and flowers all around. "Draken!" She shouted out. "Be reasonable!" She groaned looking around the room at the mess he left behind.

"You shouldn't have interrupted," Rikar told her, looking disappointed in her.

"Not you too?" Calista groaned.

"We are your mother's most trusted warriors, your life has always been a main concern of ours, princess." Rikar spoke calmly although she could hear the censor in his voice. No jovial words or mischievous grins. "How can we do our job if you don't let us? We don't know this male that you are so staunchly defending. What we do know is that we would lay down our lives for you."

"Rikar," Calista pleaded but he left as well, minus the water whirlwind thankfully.

"What did you do to Draken and Rikar?" There by the heavy drapes stood Eon, looking at her accusingly.

"And the hits keep coming," Calista muttered under her breath before moving towards her brother, stopping when he backed away from her with a glare. "Eon, I didn't do anything to them except stop them from hurting someone they knew nothing about."

"It's their job to protect you, how can they do that if you don't let them?" Eon frowned at her.

"This is why I chose to live with the mortals." Calista couldn't keep the aggravation from her voice. "I'm capable of defending myself, why can't anyone understand that?" Eon's face darkened at her words and she felt a pang of remorse, moving towards him again; she wasn't sure what she was going to do but she hated him being upset with her. Before she had even moved three feet he vortexed out of there, his vortex knocking over vases and statues before it closed in on itself. Something that she knew was on purpose, not once during any of the other vortexes he created, did he ever do such a thing.

"Is this normal?"

She turned to see Kaine watching her from the other side of the room. She gave a rueful nod. "Unfortunately, it is."

"A bit overprotective, aren't they?"

She crossed her arms, giving him a hard stare. "That is what family does and I hope that, whatever the reason you're here for, it was worth upsetting them."

"Only you can answer that." She frowned at his words but he looked around the room that looked as if a storm had swept through, which is kind of what happened. "How about we take a walk and discuss why I'm here?" he suggested. She paused, narrowing her eyes at him. "You were the one who stood up for me, I didn't ask you to. I thought you wanted to know why I was here."

Taking a deep breath, she looked around then

nodded at him. "You're right, let's go for a walk before they cool down and decide to come ask their own questions."

His brow raised. "You think they will be back after leaving like that?"

She lifted a shoulder and grinned. "As I said, we're family, and that is what family does. They'll be back; I will apologize, and then next time we will go through it all over again."

Kaine's expression clouded momentarily, his lips pursed as he slowly nodded his head. "Solen mentioned something like that, I thought he was funning me."

Calista laughed. "Nope, he was quite serious."

"I see that now." Kaine's rueful response pulled more laughter. "How about that walk?" This time she nodded.

"So, how come not only weren't you surprised to see me, but you knew my name?" Kaine asked her as they moved past the city of Atlantis into the rural area. She was careful to go the opposite direction of the caves, knowing full well that was a line she didn't dare cross. Strangers weren't allowed in the caves and regardless of her dream, he was still a stranger. She would garner more than just the brother's ire if she attempted to take Kaine there, so it was the opposite way they went.

Running her fingers along one of the colorful reef

formations, she told him about her dream, watching his eyes widen when she described the power emanating from his hands. Then the pallor of his skin dulled when she described the flash of light. Then her and Solen falling into each other's arms. "Your expression doesn't show the shock I expected; horror but no shock." Her stomach clenched with those words.

"Solen being reckless with his life? Unfortunately, no. That is why I'm here."

"What do you mean?" She frowned, not liking the sound of that.

He stopped, turned to look at her. "If not for the prophecy that brought me here, as well as the fact that you described my powers perfectly, I would think that your dream was nothing more than a woman missing her man."

"Prophecy?"

Kaine looked up to the top of the magic dome that protected all of Atlantis as if it had all the answers. "Where I come from, there is one who speaks with the spirit of our world, who sees into the future and hears prophecies that our people need to know."

"And what prophecy was told that sent you here?" Calista watched him, the images from the dream still vibrant in her mind.

Kaine looked at her. "You remember Aesis and her people?" Calista nodded, how could she forget the ones who turned the tide of the battle with the Ancients.

Without them, the battle could've ended in a whole different way. "For many years they worked with Solen to free Champions that were being held against their will by the Ancients." Calista nodded; she knew when Solen left that was his goal. She had just not expected it to take so long. "Aesis was summoned home along with those that were helping Solen."

"So, Solen couldn't rescue anymore of the Champions?"

Kaine raised a brow at her. "If you believe that, then you don't know my brother very well."

"Brother?" Calista was sure that part wasn't brought up in her dream.

Kaine let out a hearty laugh at her look of confusion. "I call him my brother, but he is in fact my best friend."

"Ahhhhhh." Calista nodded in understanding. "So, what did he do after Aesis was summoned home?"

"He kept fighting, even when the odds were against him." He nodded when Calista's eyes went wide. "The Champions that he freed joined him in battle but that still wasn't enough. There were more Ancients than he thought. It felt as if each Ancient that was conquered, more would come to take its place. We were beginning to feel hopeless, as if no matter what we did, it wouldn't matter. No one felt this pain more than Solen." Calista felt her chest tighten at his words, how she wished she could've been there for Solen. "Solen then started to get reckless, taking on battles he knew he wouldn't be able to win. When he came home with wounds that had him in a fever for days, we worried we had lost him. That was when I was told of the prophecy by our mystic."

"Mystic?"

"On our world, a mystic is one who can speak with the planet, see the future and hear the prophecies that our people need to survive. She is the one who told me that I needed to come to you."

"Me?"

Kaine nodded. "She said that Solen's recklessness will only grow until one day his luck will run out, unless the one who holds his heart is brought about." He gave a hapless shrug. "Her words, not mine. Basically, I need you to calm Solen down before he gets himself killed."

"Let me get this straight." Calista held up her hand, to which Kaine nodded and waited for her to continue. "You need me to leave my home world and go with you into space to keep Solen from doing something completely stupid and ending up dead? Did I miss anything?"

Kaine gave a slight nod of his head. "Well, there is the part where you get my company for the trip. I know many ladies who would do anything for that opportunity."

Calista stared at him, just blinking for a minute while shaking her head in disbelief. "I don't know how it is that you and the brothers aren't hitting it off. You all have the same over inflated egos." She couldn't help but to roll her eyes.

"Does that mean you're coming with me?" Kaine said, waiting for her response.

"I think that is something that needs to be discussed with the whole family." Calista whirled around to see her father, mother, grandfather, grandmother, uncles, and aunts all standing there with expressions that showed great displeasure. Fighting with the brothers was one thing, but her whole family? Eon moved out from behind her father with his arms crossed, still looking cross with her. She should've known her brother had something up his sleeve when he vortexed from her temple.

CHAPTER 5

"No way should we allow anyone to go with this alien!" Cael spoke with such force that took Calista by surprise, she knew her father could be protective of her but she had never heard him sound so discourteous to one he barely knew.

"How do we even know this male is who he says he is?" Draken asked. When they arrived at her grandparent's temple where everyone was gathered for the meeting, the dragon brothers were there waiting. She was glad that they had Kaine wait out in the courtyard while the matter was being discussed.

"I want to know why Solen wouldn't come himself," Rikar spoke up from beside his brother. Neither brother looked at Calista when they spoke, something that made her regret her words but she knew that she would do the same thing over again if it came to it. They meant well and she knew that but that didn't always excuse their overbearingness.

"Do we really owe these beings anything?" Vesper asked, looking at his fingernails.

"They did join and help us in the war with the

Ancients when we needed," his sister pointed out to him, slapping at his hands to get his attention. He just yawned.

Calista looked over at her mother who was sitting quietly and calmly at her father's side, watching Calista but saying nothing. She knew that meant her mother was contemplating all the moves of everyone on the playing field, just like she did in all her wars. Trying to minimize the casualties and still claim a victory.

"Atlantis hasn't been embroiled in any type of wars for so long, do we truly want to delve into this one?" Atmos looked to his father, Tylaos.

Tylaos, who had been listening and watching the discussion, looked to Malis. "Daughter, have you nothing to say?"

Malis smiled, still watching Calista. "Actually, Father, I was wondering what my daughter had to say about this."

For a moment, Calista wasn't sure what to say. She hadn't expected anyone to ask what she wanted, but then again, she should've known better. While the menfolk liked to try to go overboard in protecting those they love, her mother was always the calm one who wanted to know all the information before stating her opinion.

"Cali?" her mother prompted her.

Taking a deep breath, Calista spoke, "I've learned that everything happens for a reason and I believe my dream and Kaine coming here isn't coincidental."

"Whose to say that he didn't plant it?" Salis, the God of Agriculture and Inspiration, questioned.

"Because that isn't his power," Calista protested.

"How do you know that?" Rowena, who had been mostly silent, asked her.

"My dream."

"If he planted that dream, he could've planted that as well," Rowena countered.

Before Calista could dispute Rowena's words, not that she was sure how she was going to, her grandfather stood at the head of the table and everyone went silent. He looked over at Shaylane, who was sitting next to her father quietly. "Shaylane, have you had any visions that would help us with this discussion?"

"I wish I had an answer for you, Tylaos," Shaylane spoke with reverence to the God of Time and Technology. "My visions of late have been erratic, not making much sense."

"Is my granddaughter in them?" he asked her.

Shaylane nodded.

"What is her role in your visions?"

"The same as she was in my mother's," Shaylane told him. "She is the key to the Ancients' demise, but while she is here on Earth, they thrive." With her words the whole room erupted in arguments, everyone talking over one another.

"You can't expect me to let my daughter go to another planet!" Cael protested.

"We don't owe anyone anything, especially when what they want is one of our own." Atmos shook his head.

"We fought the Ancients already and sent them packing." Rikar crossed his arms.

"Actually, it was the Criptines who sent them packing," Brax spoke up for the first time since the meeting started, surprising Calista with his comment. He shrugged at the dirty looks sent his way. "I'm just stating facts."

Malis stared at her daughter silently, her eyes bright with emotion. She stood up, held out her hands to silence the protests that were about to erupt over Brax's words. She looked at Stratos who was watching everything unfold in front of him. "Stratos, what is your opinion on all this?"

"My duty is to Atlantis, and Atlantis only." Stratos spoke, causing Calista's father, Draken and Rikar to look smug. Until his next words, that was. "While the battle stays in the stars, it has nothing to do with Atlantis." He looked at Shaylane. "But if Calista stays here, will the battle stay in the stars or come to her?"

Just as the room was about to erupt in more protests and shouts, Tylaos stood up and brought his staff down on the ground, pausing everyone in time. Except him. "Enough!" He looked around the room and when it became clear that everyone had settled down, albeit rather reluctantly, he released them all. Looking at

Calista, he smiled fondly at her. "Granddaughter, you're not a youngling who can't make up their own mind." He paused in speaking to send looks towards her father and the brothers who seemed like they might protest. When he was satisfied, they weren't going to, he finished speaking. "Whether or not it will bring the battle to our doors again, this decision is yours to make. If you don't want to go, then no one will be able to force you, but if this is a trip you want to make, then you will go with my blessing."

Calista swallowed hard, knowing she was about to upset four of the most important men in her life, but this was her life. "Thank you, Grandfather." Looking around the room, she addressed them all. "You are all my family and I love you all dearly. But this is something I need to do, this is my life and my choice. I choose to go with Kaine to space and help in the battle with the Ancients."

Draken rose and the sound of his chair smashing into the wall behind him echoed around the room. Calista winced as he stormed out, slamming the mighty doors as if they weren't pure stone but rather two cheap slabs of wood. Rikar's expression was guarded and her father was scowling. She knew when Eon heard what had happened, he would show her his displeasure as well.

"Very well." Her grandfather spoke as if no chair had been thrown or doors slammed. "Give us this night to say our goodbyes and make sure that you are properly prepared for this journey. As well as giving any that might feel the need, the chance to have a chat with your traveling companion." With those words, he moved from the table and out of the room.

Poor Kaine, Calista thought with a groan.

Her father walked up to her and she braced for his reaction. "I don't like it," he said. "But I don't have to like it, to support you in your choices." He kissed her forehead and pulled her into his arms for a big hug. "Just make sure you come back to me, baby girl," he whispered in her hair.

"I will, Dad," she promised and she meant it.

"Let's get you packed with some necessities and frivolous things from home." Her mother smiled, pulling her father with her as she left. Calista nodded and attempted to follow but Shaylane approached her.

"Calista, can I have a moment please?"

Calista nodded and they moved out of the main room into the courtyard of her grandparents' temple. "What's up?"

Shaylane turned to face her, after looking around to make sure there was no one about. "I didn't want to speak in front of everyone, but I needed to warn you." Calista nodded, not sure what to say. "Mother said you were the key to destroying the Ancients but that it would come at a great price."

Calista's hand went to her pendant around her neck. "I've already paid a great price, now it's their turn."

Shaylane gave a sad shake of her head. "Mother couldn't see what that price was, or if she did, she never told me. I've been trying to look and see but my vision is cloudy. I hear your wails and feel your pain though, it has kept me up at night." A lone tear escaped and slowly slid down her cheek.

"Are you trying to tell me not to go?" Calista wasn't so sure now, hearing this.

Hastily wiping away the tear, Shaylane shook her head. "I wish I could but no, you must go or else the fight will come here to Atlantis, and if it does, we all lose."

"Okay, anything else you want to bring with you? Maybe a spare table, bed or set of chairs?" Kaine asked after sending up the fifth load of supplies her family had gathered for them. She had spent the night with her family, saying their goodbyes and promising to return home as swiftly as possible. Her brother Eon, nor Draken, or Rikar could be found, she hated that they were still mad at her but that was something she would deal with when she returned.

She didn't know if anyone had spoken with Kaine, as her grandfather had implied yesterday. He hadn't said anything and she wasn't asking.

Calista laughed, "Yeah, they might've gone a bit overboard, but they are just being helpful."

Kaine snorted. "Clori keeps grumbling about torching the next thing that comes up if it isn't us."

Calista frowned. "Clori? That name sounds familiar."

"It should." Calista whipped her head towards him. "She said she knew you."

"Hmmmm."

Kaine laughed, "No worries, you will be able to get reacquainted when we get aboard my ship."

"Well, I've said my goodbyes." Calista grimaced. "At least to those who weren't avoiding me."

"I'm sorry about causing you grief within your family." Kaine truly looked repentant.

"Not your fault." Calista shrugged. "My family just tends to be overprotective, when I get home we will settle it all."

"Why wait until then?"

Calista turned around with a smile seeing Rikar and Draken both standing there. She ran and leapt into their arms hugging them. "You came to see me off!"

"Not exactly." Rikar gave Kaine a hard stare.

"Rikar, you guys aren't going to give Kaine a hard time," Calista told him, her foot stomping down in emphasis. Something that wasn't lost on Rikar whose lips twisted in a smirk. "I mean it."

"Relax, princess," Rikar told her. "Not going to give anyone a hard time."

"So, what did you mean by not exactly?" Calista looked up at him.

"We're going with you," Draken said in a stern voice. That wasn't what she expected to hear.

Before she could say anything Kaine raised a brow. "You're going with us?" His voice was telling how much of a bad idea he thought that was.

Draken leveled him with one of his hard stares. "If Calista is going, then yes, we're going too."

Kaine looked between the brothers and Calista before shrugging. "Look, I don't care who is going but we need to do just that, go. We have wasted enough time already." He moved forward, taking out a slim silver box from his coat pocket.

"I'm coming too!" They all turned to see Eon standing there with a bag packed and a stubborn expression on his face.

"There are no babysitters where we're going," Kaine spoke, his voice laced with aggravation.

Eon glared at him. "I don't need no babysitter! And if my sister, Rikar and Draken are going, then so am I!"

"Eon," Calista attempted to reason with him. "You can't go, you're needed here with Mom and Dad. I promise I won't be gone long." She attempted to embrace him but he jerked back from her, looking at the brothers.

"Draken, Rikar, tell them I'm going as well. You guys will need me to help make sure nothing happens to my sister," he pleaded.

Rikar ruffled his hair. "Sorry, little time turner, but this is a trip you can't make with us."

"Draken!" Eon implored the one he idolized, hoping he would back him up.

"No!" Only one word, but with Draken, there was only one ever needed. Eon's eyes started to water up and his lip trembled slightly.

"Eon," Calista implored, reaching for him but he vortexed out before she could reach him. Sighing, she turned to Draken. "Couldn't you have put that in a nicer way, let him down gently?"

"I'll make it up to him when we return, coddling him was only delaying the inevitable and as your friend said, we've wasted enough time as is." Draken stared at her. "Unless your friend is lying."

She gave a frustrated growl, moving to stand next to Kaine. "Let's get going, but you will be making it up to him."

Kaine looked between the three of them as if he was second guessing this trip, which she couldn't blame him, before giving a small shake of his head. "Okay, then, let's go." With that, he pushed a button on the silver box and the world around them lit up brightly.

CHAPTER 6

"Hey Clori!" Kaine smiled at the very Amazon looking woman who greeted them. Her fiery red hair falling in waves of flames, her skin bronze as if kissed by the sun and her golden eyes turning to Calista who gasped.

"You!" Calista pointed at her; mouth open as she remembered the female. "You were there when I first met Shaylane!"

Clori inclined her head, speaking in her masculine voice, "Guilty."

Calista turned to the brothers who were giving her odd looks. "That's right, you weren't there." She pressed her lips together then just laughed. "Draken, Rikar, meet Clori. She was one of the Champions who fought with us."

Draken nodded to her while Rikar moved forward with that dashing grin of his that foretold he was about to lay down a line, one that he thought was a good one. "Hello, fire angel. Let me know when you need some help putting on sunscreen."

Clori raised a fiery brow at him. "I don't use sunscreen."

"That's okay, neither do I."

Clori laughed. "I have to admit, you're nice on the eyes and I love your energy, but I seriously don't think you can handle the heat when it comes to me."

"I'd be willing to try." Rikar, grinned pooling water in his hand, water that went flying when Calista slapped him.

"Enough!" She rolled her eyes at him but he just winked back. "You're incorrigible."

"Thank you."

She gave him a baleful look before turning to Kaine. "Didn't you say something about a tour?" Her lips pressed together as both brothers laughed. Figures Draken would laugh at that.

Clori grinned. "They haven't changed much."

Calista groaned and looked at Kaine imploring him to move past this. "Tour?"

"The lady wants a tour. Clori, let's give her one." Kaine sounded more amused than she cared for but thankfully he started down the corridor. "Besides, if we sit in the cargo bay too long, Arlo might just open the back doors on us."

"He does get particular about anyone lingering in his cargo bay," Clori agreed then grinned at Calista. "He also had some choice words for all the supplies that you sent up." Calista winced but Clori laughed. "That's all right, although I was surprised you didn't send a kitchen sink."

Calista stopped short, staring at Clori whose brow furrowed looking back at her. "What's wrong?"

"That is an Earth saying."

Clori frowned. "And?"

"How do you know Earth lingo? Have you been here since last I saw you?"

"Ahhhhh." Clori nodded. "Now I understand. This is the first time I've been back since leaving with Solen all those years ago. How I picked up the lingo... we have an Earth specialist on board who loves to quiz us on all she knows."

"Continuously." Kaine groaned.

Clori snorted. "Like you have room to talk, you and your military exercises."

"Hey!" Kaine protested. "Those are useful and have saved your sorry ass many times."

"So, how's Shaylane doing?" Clori ignored Kaine, asking Calista, who was about to answer when Rikar darted by them into the shadows. When he came out from the shadows, he wasn't alone. In his grasp was a dark woman whose skin glinted in the hallway lights. Almost as tall as Rikar, staring defiantly at him with dark eyes that had a silver circle around the center when he shoved her into the wall. Her long black hair was woven into many small braids that trailed down past her waist, hair that stayed still even during the tussle.

"Who are you?" Rikar gritted out between his teeth.

The world around Calista felt as if it had almost

slowed down in time. Clori's whole body started to tense up and glow as her eyes narrowed on Rikar. Draken's eyes went full dragon, his body glowing as he watched Clori and Kaine. Kaine's hands glowed as he went on defense mode as well, which didn't help the tension ease within Calista. She was remembering the scene from her dream, where Kaine placed his glowing hands on the ground, sending power streaking all around and exploding.

"Rikar!" she shouted to the brother that had always been the more relaxed and playful one, this was a side she rarely saw, if at all. She placed herself between the others and Rikar, hoping that might pause any thoughts of retaliation towards him. "Let that person go."

"I'll ask you one more time, who are you?" Rikar demanded again, his body starting to glow as his dragon was just beneath the surface. What had gotten into him? Calista wasn't sure what was going on as she stood there with four powerful beings all on the defense.

"Her name is Livinia," Kaine bit out. "She is part of my crew and, unlike you or your brother, she was invited."

"Why was she lurking in the shadows and watching us as if waiting to strike?" Rikar refused to look away from Livinia who was staring back at him with the same defiant look, her back straight and no signs that Rikar's actions had intimidated her at all.

"Her kind practically lives in the shadows." Kaine

informed him. Calista could see the sparks arcing from his fingers as they glowed brighter. "Now get your hands off my crew member before I make you." Kaine's voice was strained with his anger.

"What do you mean her kind?" Rikar asked, still holding the stoic Livinia against the wall.

"Livinia is a Cacordia from the planet Cacen." Calista could hear the impatience in Kaine's voice but she knew this wasn't like Rikar. She just wished she had known what had gotten into him.

Rikar snorted. "That still doesn't explain why she was sulking in the shadows following us."

"Her kind are assassins of the highest regard," Clori spoke since Kaine didn't seem willing to disclose any more information. "They are sought after for their ability to blend in anywhere, with any kind. That and their reputation for always getting their mark, mainly because they never stop until they do." Clori lifted a shoulder nonchalantly, although her posture showed anything but nonchalance.

"That explanation doesn't make her stalking us look good at all," Draken spoke, although his body wasn't glowing as much as earlier.

"Whether they are among friends or not, that is how they move about." Clori threw Draken an exasperated look.

Rikar turned away from Livinia, his brow furrowing at Clori. "And the reason she wouldn't answer me?" he demanded of her.

"Because I owe you nothing," the voice was low and coarse.

Rikar turned back around to face her, only to discover that she was no longer pressed against the wall. She wasn't even there. "What the?" He jerked around several times but she was nowhere to be seen.

"Oh, and the Cacordias don't really care to explain themselves." Kaine grinned at the frustration on Rikar's face. "Let's finish that tour we started."

"The next stalker will have to deal with me," Draken informed him, his expression and demeanor still rigid, but at least he still followed Kaine. Calista sent up a silent prayer that there would be no more stalkers, she wasn't sure this space craft could handle a battle of powers within.

Kaine shrugged a shoulder as he moved further into the ship, motioning to a set of double metal doors to their left. "Through those doors is engineering. You can almost always find our engineer, Bern, there making sure the ship runs up to his standards." Moving forward, he showed them the guest quarters, the hold where all the supplies her family had insisted they bring were being stored, then motioned for them to follow him up some stairs.

"Up here are the crew's quarters, galley, sick bay, weapons and specialties." Kaine said making sure to show each room as he spoke. Then they ascended one more set of stairs and entered a room that kind of resembled one of the bridges on a starship from that one science fiction movie. "Welcome to the bridge." Calista had to bite back a smile since his words aligned with her thoughts so perfectly.

There were blinking lights, dials, and colorful buttons all along the wall and the panels that stuck out from the wall several feet from the floor. Chairs that looked as if they had grown from the floor were placed along the walkway. There were two main consoles on the floor, in front of a big screen that showed the view outside, just like the view screen on the show. Seated at one of the consoles were two beings who were almost identical, their skin a translucent blue, while their hair looked like silver metal spikes. Both turned and waved at them, it was then that they saw the only visible difference. One had grey eyes while the other had purple. "Meet Clyde and Clare, they are the best navigators you will find in any solar system."

Calista nodded, then turned when Kaine introduced them to Stryx, who was the pilot seated at the other console in front of the screen. Hair as red as fire, eyes as green as jade and sharp as a knife, he barely acknowledged them as he nodded slightly in their direction. Fingers moving across the console in front of him, lights blinking beneath each touch. "Tanis, our medic, is probably in sick bay with our weapon specialist, Allie." Kaine grinned. "No worries, you'll meet them soon enough."

"Don't forget about Lissy," Clori said as she sat

down in one of the three chairs that were situated in the center of the bridge. There was one that was just a bit higher up than the other two that were situated on either side. It was the one on the left that Clori was now seated in.

"How could I forget about our Earth specialist?" Kaine chuckled. "And you already know my first mate, Clori."

"Interesting crew you have," Draken spoke as his gaze swept the room around them.

Kaine nodded. "Yes, they are."

"Seems to have a multiple of races." Rikar looked around the room then back at Kaine.

"Very observant." Kaine moved to take his seat in the chair that was the highest of the three. "Everyone on this ship was once a Champion that was enslaved by the Ancients. Freed by Solen in one of the many battles he fought since he left your planet. They owe their freedom to Solen and, although he told them they were free to do as they pleased, they wanted to join him in his quest to free the universe from the tyranny of the Ancients."

"Now if we can just keep him from destroying himself," Stryx muttered as he ran two fingers down the console, lights blinking in the exact path his fingers moved.

"What do you mean?" Rikar frowned.

"Solen's been getting a bit … reckless in his battles with the Ancients," Kaine said with a grimace.

"Reckless?" Clori raised a brow at him. "That's putting it mildly."

"How about you quit putting it mildly and just spit it out." Draken glowered at Kaine. "I was of the understanding that you were sent by Solen for help in dealing with the Ancients." His glare moved to Calista who pressed her lips together.

"Actually, Solen doesn't know he is here," she admitted.

"Princess?" Rikar's frown deepened.

She sighed, "Aesis was summoned home and in her absence Solen was getting reckless. Their mystic said I was the only one who could save him from himself."

"Why didn't you say that during the counsel at your grandparent's?" Draken asked.

Calista snorted, "I knew I was going to have a hard enough time just saying Solen needed help, if I told everyone about Solen being reckless, they would've attempted to stop me from leaving."

"With good reason." Rikar crossed his arms. "Going to help in battle is one thing but helping when someone is being reckless with their own life is suicidal."

"I'm not going to abandon him." Calista spoke with the same force as Rikar. She needed them to understand this wasn't something she could be talked out of.

"We're going home, now!" Draken told her, moving forward and pulling her closer.

"That's going to be a bit hard," Kaine told them as

he looked down at a panel that appeared from the arm of the chair he was sitting in.

Draken snorted, "You think I can't shimmer us from this ship back to Earth?"

Kaine looked over at him. "If we were still in Earth's atmosphere, maybe. But we're light years from Earth. You attempt to shimmer back to Earth and you can end up stuck in a void that you won't be able to return from." He pushed a button on the panel. "If I were you, I'd relax and enjoy the ride. Explore your first space-ship." He suggested. "We still have several hours before we are able to space fold."

"Space fold?" Rikar frowned, turning to look at the view screen.

"It would take centuries to reach our planet without folding, we don't have that long," Kaine told him. "Bern will let us know when it's time to get ready for the deep sleep."

"Deep sleep?" Draken's face darkened.

Kaine looked over at him. "When this ship folds, if any of us are still in a state of flux, then our bodies will come apart. When the ship unfolds, there will be nothing but shreds of us left on the floor." He winked at Calista who couldn't contain the look of horror at that thought. "No worries, Spider, I won't let you come apart at the seams. Solen would kill me."

"I don't think it's him you need to worry about right now." Draken glowered.

"No worries, Bern will have the stability pods ready before the fold. We will go into a deep sleep, our minds and bodies will be protected within these pods," Kaine assured him.

"And why should we trust you?" Rikar asked.

Kaine shrugged. "Trust me or don't, get in the pods or don't, I could care less," he told them. "My mission was to bring Calista to Solen, you two are your own responsibility."

Calista stood there watching and she had finally had enough. "I don't know why you three can't get along, but I've had enough of this." She turned to look at Draken and Rikar with her hands on her hips. "You both invited yourselves on this journey and you'll start behaving as such." Then she turned to Kaine, who was smirking. "You were the one who came to me, and whether you like it or not, they are my family. If all you're going to do is bait them, then the next time they go dragon I might let them drown you." With that she stalked off the bridge, not even paying attention to the three sets of male eyes that followed her with admiration.

"She's got spunk, I see why Solen likes her." Kaine chuckled.

"You should see her when she gets really riled." Rikar nodded.

CHAPTER 7

Calista found a seat in the galley that was situated right by a window that let her see outside the ship. Never once in all the many years of her life had she ever imagined that she would travel in space. Leaning her forehead against the cool glass, she just stared into the emptiness of space, her mind wandering. She couldn't help but think about the day she had met Solen all those years ago. She wondered if he still wore that long leather jacket.

"Penny for your thoughts?" Turning her head, she saw Rikar standing there in the doorway watching her.

"Might be a bit expensive."

Rikar moved to stand behind her, placing his hands on her shoulders, giving them a gentle squeeze. Leaning over he looked at her with a grin from his upside-down face. "You know us dragons, we have our own hoards of treasures, I'm sure I can afford it."

She tried to keep the smile at bay but by the smirk on his face she could tell that it was obvious. Reaching out she grabbed his hair that was hanging down and gave it a tug. "Brat," she affectionately scolded.

Laughing, Rikar flipped over her and landed on the chair across from her. "You still love me." The smile that she flashed turned into a grimace at what he said next. "You and every girl that meets me." His teeth flashed as he grinned at her.

"Really? Explain Clori." She enjoyed bursting that over inflated comment, although she should've known that he'd have something to come back with.

"She just wants me to chase her." Rikar blew on his nails. "I haven't decided if I want to accommodate the lady yet."

"Even after all these years, I'm still amazed that you are able to walk through doorways with that over inflated ego of yours." Calista gave a shake of her head.

Rikar's jovial expression turned serious, something that only happened when he had something to say that you had better listen to. "You know Draken loves you, right?"

Calista sighed, she had wondered if they were going to have a talk about this. Of course, it should be her and Draken, not her and Rikar. Except that Draken shared the same ideology that their resident assassin did, he refused to explain himself to anyone, no matter the relationship. Taking a deep breath she answered him, "I have to admit that since you guys got back from your father's, I've had my doubts."

"Awww, princess," Rikar's voice cajoled as he reached out to place his hand on top of hers. "You have to know that he does. I wish I could tell you why he changed, but it's not really my story to tell."

Yanking her hand from his, she stood up. "No, it's his and he should be the one trying to talk to me, not you." She had spent the time since the brothers got back from their father's internally explaining Draken's brusque change of attitude with her so as to not be hurt by it, and doing her best to not feel as if she had become one of his many throwaways. But no matter how many times she attempted to rationalize the hurt she felt or his attitude towards her, it never truly helped. "He was the one who stopped caring about me, he was the one who started treating me as one of his past flings and he can be the one to explain to me why." With those words she turned and marched out of the room, ignoring Rikar's pleading voice to come back and talk to him.

This was the first time either one of the brothers had ever brought it up, her mother and father had tried to help her understand the change in the man she called brother for so long but even they didn't truly know what to say. No one knew what happened. Fine, Draken didn't want anyone to know what happened, then Draken could take his over protectiveness and shove it down that arrogant throat of his. That thought was punctuated with a side kick to an empty metal drum that just happened to be near her. The sound of it tumbling down the hallway and then down the stairs echoed loudly, bringing a grimace to her face.

"Is that how the gods and goddesses of Earth vent frustrations? Or, is that a new kind of game?" Kaine startled her, coming from the sick bay.

Calista felt her cheeks burn. "Sorry." She looked down sheepishly. "Just a small temper tantrum. Won't happen again. Promise."

"Can you truly promise that?"

She frowned at him. "What exactly did Solen tell you about me?"

"Enough for me to know that you can't make that promise in good faith." His tone held no censor but there was humor in his eyes.

She let out a big breath. "No, I can't."

Kaine's bark of laughter brought a smile to her face, one that was truly needed at this time. "C'mon Spider, walk with me down to the cargo hold so I can make sure everything is strapped down and ready for space fold."

She looked sideways at him. "Thought Arlo had issues with people being in his cargo bay?"

"Nah, just when they loiter down there, as he calls it." One of Kaine's muscular shoulders moved up in a dismissive manner. "Making sure everything is strapped down so as not to do any damage? He won't get testy about that."

"Okay, but if I end up out in space, I won't be able to protect you from the brothers' ire," she informed him with a quirk of her lips.

"No worries." With those words he grabbed the railing and vaulted over, landing on his feet down below. He looked up at her with a grin. "You coming?"

Not to be outdone, she took her pointer finger and placed it on the top of the railing. Raising her body slowly she rolled over the railing, letting herself slowly lower to the ground below until her feet gently touched and she stood next to Kaine who was curling his lip at her.

"Show off," he grumbled at her as she laughed. "Let's go." Still laughing, she followed him into the cargo bay. She looked around for the metal drum as they walked, but it was nowhere to be seen. She was sure it had bounced down the stairs, she wondered if Arlo had taken care of the drum.

"What happened to make you worry about Solen?" Calista asked Kaine as she was helping with attaching clamps and putting up shields in the cargo bay. "You said he was becoming reckless." She prompted.

"During our last battle, we were fighting the Ancients and their Champions like normal, when suddenly he seemed distracted. One of the Champions got a good shot in with an energy pulse, taking Solen down. I had to cause a distraction so we could escape," he answered her.

"How'd you do that?" She asked him.

"I energized the terrain around us so that it exploded, giving us cover to get out of there." Kaine strapped down some containers that were hanging on the wall. "Stryx played hell maneuvering the ship to pick us up and get us out of there. After conferring with our mystic, we learned about the prophecy. At first we laughed it off until we found Solen attempting to gather a team for another run against the Ancients."

"Why does that make him reckless? Isn't that the goal?"

Kaine snorted. "He was still healing but he had taken off the bandages so he could get into his fighting gear. He could barely stand straight but he was heading into battle again." Kaine leaned back against the wall, looking at her. "That was when we realized the mystic's prophecy was indeed real."

Calista mulled over what he said, the description of the battle resembled her dream the other night. Well, her nightmare. Could that have been the case? Was her dream just her seeing what was happening with Solen? She was about to mention that to Kaine when a crackling sound came through the speakers overhead.

"20 minutes to fold coordinates, ready positions." Clori's voice could be heard above the static.

"Nap time." Kaine winked. "Let's get you comfortable."

Waking up in the sleep pod, Calista almost forgot

where she was. That was until Kaine leaned over the top, grinning down through the glass at her. Getting out of the pod, she looked around only to see that it was just Kaine, Draken, Rikar, and herself in the room. "Are we here?" She asked, her heart beating faster thinking about seeing Solen again after all these years.

Kaine nodded as the brothers moved to stand beside her. Smiling appreciatively at them she turned to Kaine. "So, let's go have a talk with Mr. Reckless."

"You know, now that I have you here, I'm starting to wonder if this was such a good idea," Kaine mused. "Not sure I'll survive Solen's ire."

"Tough." Calista snorted, moving to the doorway. "Let's go, I've waited long enough."

"You heard the princess," Rikar quipped, following along grinning broadly while Kaine groaned.

"Kaine! There you are, Solen's been asking where you were. It's been hard to keep him distracted." They had just disembarked from the ship, Calista and the brothers were staring around at the new world around them when the petite, slender female came rushing to Kaine. Her soft lavender colored hair flowed all around her, almost reaching the ground. Her purplish eyes that matched her hair widened upon seeing them standing there, her steps faltering as she reached Kaine, although her gaze zoomed on Calista.

"Hi." Calista raised a hand in greeting, but the female barely acknowledged her as she turned back to Kaine.

"Who are the spares?" Rikar and Draken both growled at her words which seemed to startle her as she took a step back, frowning at them. "I didn't mean to offend; I just wasn't expecting him to bring anyone else."

Draken snorted in disbelief while Rikar's look darkened, although to Calista's surprise they both stayed silent. Though neither moved from her flank, something that she appreciated right now.

"Calista, Rikar, Draken," Kaine spoke to them then gestured to the female before them. "Meet Lizbet, our resident mystic."

Calista nodded as Lizbet gave a smile that didn't quite reach her eyes, the brothers just grunted.

"Where's Solen?" Kaine asked.

"Wondering where the hell you have been."

Turning Calista felt as if she had been knocked to the ground, breathless as she stared at the man who haunted her thoughts and dreams. Solen. His dark eyes were boring right into Kaine, he hadn't noticed her and the brothers yet. His hair was a bit longer than she remembered but still dark as it fell around his face.

She watched him, the world around her disappearing, the only thing she saw or heard was Solen. She took a hesitant step forward, that was when Solen turned and saw her standing there. If she hadn't been so awed at seeing him, she might have laughed when he stumbled in surprise. All she knew was that he never looked better. "Solen!" She rushed to him, jumping into his arms that wrapped around her, holding her to him. Her cheeks were wet with the tears that were running freely but she didn't care, she was in his arms at last.

"Spider! How?" He breathed as he looked down at her, his eyes full of amazement and joy.

Pulling his head down she kissed him, enjoying the feeling as he held her to him, deepening the kiss as they forgot about everything else but each other. She didn't know how long they stood there in each other's arms, but the sound of several throats clearing finally brought them out of their own little world they were in. She smiled up at him. "I love you." She told him.

"And I love you." He leaned down to kiss her again.

THWACK!

CHAPTER 8

"What the Hades was that for?" Solen rubbed his chin that was already starting to glow red from Calista's punch. Calista heard Lizbet's gasp but she refused to look away from Solen.

"That was for not coming home sooner." Calista folded her arms glaring at him.

"Missed you too, Spider." Solen pulled the petulant Calista into his arms, she resisted for a moment before allowing him to hold her to him. "I'm sorry," he murmured into her hair. "I never expected to be gone so long."

Those words had Calista pulling back and looking up at him critically. Her fingers brushed along the darkening skin on his chin. He grinned at her. "It doesn't hurt."

"That's not what I was thinking." She smirked at his frown, then grew serious again. "You have barely aged but yet it has been centuries upon centuries since you've been gone."

"Did you want me to age?" Grinning down at her, his smile slipped when she didn't return the gesture. He gave a sigh, "It's a long story but I promise to explain, well, the best I can."

"You better." She emphasized each word with a chest poke.

"You gave in way too quickly there, princess." Rikar shook his head at her. "You should've let him dangle a lot longer than that."

Solen turned to Rikar and Draken, who were watching them, his eyes lighting up at seeing them. Rikar grinned, moving forward to clasp Solen's hand like an old friend, while Draken stayed back, scowling at Solen. "Wouldn't worry too much about big brother, he's just sore that Calista did what he wanted."

"Actually, she didn't." Draken moved forward, holding out a hand staring at Solen. "You're still standing."

Solen clasped Draken's hand with a grin, pulling him to warp an arm around his neck, joyed to see his friend. Though Calista could see the wariness in his eyes. "Good to see you too, brother."

Draken snorted. "Make Calista cry again and I'm burying you."

"Draken!" Calista protested, not sure if she was protesting the violence against Solen or just shocked at hearing the protectiveness in his voice that she hadn't heard in a long time when it came to her.

Solen gently jerked her to him, kissing her hair. "That's all right, Spider. He has every reason to threaten me."

"Good, he can threaten you instead of me now." Kaine grinned watching them. "They've been giving me a hard time in your absence."

"Really?" Solen looked at Draken and Rikar. Draken nodded, his lips curling. Solen laughed, "

good."

"Hey! You jerk!" Kaine protested but Solen laughed harder.

"Dude, I'm positive you deserved it."

"He did," Calista agreed.

Kaine frowned at her. "I thought you liked me, Spider."

Solen frowned at him. "That's my nickname for her."

Kaine shrugged. "Heard you call her that so much, it's more natural to think of her as Spider than Calista."

"Well, you can call her Calista." Solen held her closer, frowning at Kaine. "She's my Spider."

Kaine held out his hands in surrender. "All yours, mate." He took two steps back.

Calista watched them from Solen's arms, feeling happy and safe for the first time in a long time. As they joked, Calista felt as if they were being watched. She looked around but didn't see anyone, that was when she realized that Lizbet had disappeared.

Kaine had taken the brothers to town so that Solen and Calista could have some quality time without any onlookers. Hands linked together; Calista leaned into Solen's side with her head on his shoulder and one hand on his arm, they walked past where the ship loomed over the land. The land that was unlike anything Calista had seen. The terrain was that of grassy hills, bushes, flora, and just a bit farther there was a forest of trees. Although the grass was a rainbow of muted colors, as well as the trees and bushes all around. The view was beautiful, the sky a soft mixture of pastel colors with a breeze that was warm and welcoming.

"Meet Ara." Solen gestured all around them.

"Ara?"

"Ara is our world, as Gaia is yours," Solen explained.

Calista looked around her at all the colors on the trees, bushes, flora and terrain all around them. Her lips curled into a soft smile, her head tilting as she looked up to Solen. "She's beautiful."

"Thank you."

Calista looked around, trying to find the source of the small squeaky voice that she just heard, but there was no one but them there. She frowned up at Solen who was grinning broadly at her look of confusion. "You heard that, right?" He nodded, which had her looking around again. When she still came up empty handed with no answer, her gaze turned to Solen, once again. "I'm not going crazy!" Her voice rose slightly.

"No, Spider, you're not going crazy." Solen agreed, explaining. "What you heard was an Aggie."

"Aggie? Who is she? Or better yet, where is she?" Calista asked.

"Aggie isn't a person, more like a race." Calista opened her mouth to say something but was unable to form any words so she closed it. "Let me see if I can explain it better than that." Solen gave an awkward laugh.

"Please do." Calista watched him.

"Aggies are considered the children of Ara."

Calista frowned. "Aren't you all?"

"In a way." Solen sighed and looked up into the sky with pursed lips before looking back at her with a very thoughtful expression. "Aggies are born directly from Ara. Ara's both their mother and father, they live within Ara."

"Live within Ara?"

"In the flora, the fauna, the terrain." Solen gestured with each word. "There are many different types of Aggies that live in different types of terrains."

"Terrains?"

"Ecosystems." Solen grinned. "There are the Aggies that live in the forest terrain that you see around us, then the ones that live in a type of grassland, the aquatic lands as well as the freezing tundra. That is why you can't see them." He frowned when her eyes went wide as she looked past him. "Calista?" When she didn't answer him, he turned, grinning at what he saw. "Hello, Sanders. What brought you out?"

Standing there in the dirt pathway stood Sanders.

Barely three feet tall, crystal skin that glinted in the sun, big curious eyes that watched her from beneath bushy rainbow eyebrows that were tinged with white just like his long, fluffy hair that reached the ground. His clothes matched the massive tree next to him. A tree that seemed to be as old as the miniature man. "Our new visitor." His hair bobbled as he nodded towards Calista, who was just staring at him. "We wanted to meet her." He spoke in his squeaky voice that seemed to soften with his age, as it surely didn't sound as high pitched as the first one she had heard.

"We?" Calista looked around, gasping as more Aggies seemed to morph from nearby bushes, trees, flowers and even the soft purple hued grass. All with the same crystal skin, bright rainbow hair without the white edges of Sanders' age, big eyes and curious expressions. A petite female whose hair wrapped around her body; a smaller little boy who was grasping on the branch of his bush next to a male that was several inches above him. "Hello," Calista greeted them as she knelt down to their size.

The smaller child-like Aggie moved closer to her with great curiosity shining in his eyes. "Bastion." The male chided him, but the child paid him no mind as he reached out for her. Reaching out her hand, palm up, she watched as he placed his chunky crystal hand in hers. As soon as crystal touched skin, Bastion's face lit up and he smiled at her.

"Mine!" His voice squeaked out happily, bringing laughter from the others. "I claim her!"

"Find your own," Solen told him amidst the laughter.

A movement off to the side showed another smaller female who was looking at Calista curiously, pulling herself from a small green flower. "Juna!" Bastion greeted her, his hand still in Calista's. Juna nodded in greeting although her eyes never left Calista.

"I don't believe anyone has ever seen this many Aggies at one time." The amazement in Solen's voice had Calista looking up at him.

"Really?" The bemused look on Solen's face as he looked around them as more Aggies slowly appeared, watching them with great curiosity, spoke more than the slow nod he gave. Aggies of all different sizes appeared from the scenery around them and all staring at Calista with a mixture of wonder and interest. "Hello," Calista greeted them all, Bastion's hand still in hers as she knelt there on the ground looking around.

"Sanders is the leader of the woodland Aggies," Solen told her as Sanders moved closer to her. Bastion grudgingly removed his hand from hers, letting his leader closer. Although, Bastion was watching Sanders very closely.

Calista gave a respectful nod in greeting. "Hello, Sanders."

Sanders stopped barely inches from her as he looked her over, not even trying to disguise it. His wide eyes that never seemed to blink were sharp as he took in her appearance and possibly more. She wasn't sure what he was seeing but hoped that she passed inspection. It would suck to come all this way to see Solen to have these people that he seemed to have such respect for, not like her. His lips curved into a smile and he gave her a nod, which must have been a good thing since the other Aggies erupted into cheers as they clapped and jumped.

Sanders turned to Solen, gave a nod and then very nimbly leapt from his place back into the great tree that he had come from. Calista frowned as the rest of the Aggies scurried back into their respective homes, Bastion smiled at her before he fell into his bush. Calista looked to Solen. "Why are they leaving? Did I do something wrong?"

A noise that came from the trees around them caught both of their attention before Solen could answer. Turning to their right they saw Lizbet coming from those trees. "There you two are." She spoke in her soft voice, Calista wondered if maybe it was her appearance that sent the Aggies back into hiding. She didn't want to seem mean but she truly hoped that was it and that she hadn't done anything to offend the Aggies. Lizbet looked to Solen. "Father wanted me to inform you that the celebration was about to start."

Solen nodded to her. "Tell him we will be back shortly." Lizbet nodded back, gave a sideline glance in Calista's direction before disappearing into the trees.

That glance was neither friendly nor deadly, but Calista felt that she had seen it before, in a different female and different situation.

"Is there something I should know? She doesn't seem too fond of me." She asked Solen who just grabbed her hand with that grin of his.

"Only thing you should know is that I'm happy to see you and I have something else that I want to show you before I have to share you with the rest of the town." Solen pulled her along as he moved further down the trail.

"Simply gorgeous," Calista breathed as she looked out at the view before her, the puzzling attitude of Lizbet forgotten for the moment. Solen moved closer from behind, his arms wrapping around her waist as he moved to place his face next to hers.

"I love this place," he said softly into her hair. "I would come here often when I needed to clear my thoughts. I've never shared this place with anyone."

She turned to look at him, her eyes wide. "Never?"

He shook his head and smiled at her. "No."

She looked back over the view that spread out before them, past the cliff they were standing on. Foliage full of multiple colors that surrounded a beautiful water oasis with a waterfall that fell from a mountainside. Smooth rocks that cupped some of the water as it spilled into the pool below. "I can't believe that no one has ever found this place."

"I didn't say that." Solen laughed, playing with her hair as he backed away slightly. "The pool below is one of the popular recreations for my people." She frowned at him, which only made his smile widen. "I've never shared this place with anyone, and as far as I know, no one has ever found it."

"How have you kept it a secret?"

Solen nodded to a plant with wide colored leaves on it, that branched out from the ground. The leaves were green with pink and purple glistening colors that dripped down the leaves. "That plant is the Ziptuck plant, one that keeps everyone away from this area where it thrives."

"Is it poisonous?" Calista was trying to think if they had come in contact with them during their trek up here but wasn't sure.

Solen shook his head. "Not truly poisonous, but if you were to disturb them, they would emit spores that would put you into a deep sleep. So everyone stays away from here but being the excellent hunter that I am, I'm able to move through without disturbing one Ziptuck."

"So, it makes this your own private, secluded getaway," Calista mused, looking around them. Solen nodded as he watched her looking down at the pool below. "Everything looks so untouched, on Earth if there was a popular area, the evidence would be plain to see."

"We thank Ara for everything, the air we breathe, the water and food that sustain us and our very lives. Unlike your Gaia, she is a big part of our lives. Your Gaia stays in the background while Ara provides our people with not only substance to survive but each of us have a special gift." Heis hands moved cautiously over the leaves of a nearby tree. "In return we worship her as our mother and treat all around us with the respect due a mother. We take care of her and she takes care of us."

"You mean your skill as a hunter." Calista frowned at his nod. "Could she take it away?"

This question had Solen looking perplexed, something that could be heard in his words. "I don't know, it has never happened. No one has ever disrespected Ara, we have always shown her respect and in turn she has kept us safe." He looked off into the distance from where they had come from, turning to look at her and smile. "I've been selfish with your time for long enough. Time for you to meet my family and my people."

CHAPTER 9

The whole town was gathered together in the center where a bonfire was flickering in the evening air. Another new experience for Calista as she could feel the heat of the fire but could sense that the fire did no damage to the land around it. Solen told her that the fire never goes out, it is more subdued during the day time but always there. She was seated next to Solen, close to the fire. Lizbet was there as well, standing next to a slender man with silver hair that had lilac purple hues, who towered over her by at least a good foot or so. She was dressed in purple robes that had golden accents along the sleeves and waist. The man wore black slacks with a deep purple buttoned-down shirt. He seemed to have an air of importance about him as he smiled in greeting when she and Solen had arrived. She was sure he was of advanced age, although his pasty white skin was wrinkle free. Solen had introduced them when they first arrived, bowing his head towards the slender Grint in respect.

Sitting there with Solen, who had his arm around her waist, Calista pulled her legs up and leaned against him as the fire grew in size. Within the flames hues of purple and pink appeared against the dark backdrop with sparkling lights. Grint moved forward as Lizbet stayed her position, her hands clasped lightly in front of her as she watched him.

"In the beginning, there was nothing but a vast darkness all around until a light appeared, a light that grew brighter until it burst into many shards that shot out into the darkness. These shards created solar systems where only darkness had reigned. In each solar system one of the Empyrean lights would create worlds and life, choosing one world to be its own."

As the man spoke visions appeared in the fire. The visions were of the lights that he spoke about, shooting out through the darkness. It showed many different solar systems with different planets, stars, moons, asteroids, comets, and several different galaxies. Calista was staring in wonder at the sight, momentarily speechless.

"The Empyrean then created life on the world they claimed as their own, that life would worship the Empyrean, in return the Empyrean would nurture and care for them, sometimes granting gifts, whether the gifts be of a cerebral nature or physical one."

In the fire she saw many different scenes, one she could tell was Earth while the others must be from other planets. But in each one she saw people with powers, people that seemed to hold positions of power and those who followed them. In the scene of Earth, she saw herself, her grandparents and the mortals that lived their lives not believing in the myths of the past.

"Ara is our Empyrean." Grint looked towards Calista as he continued. "Gaia is yours, although I understand that your people call her Earth." Calista nodded. Grint looked back towards the fire where there were two images, one of Gaia and the other of Ara. "You could call them siblings. They had a connection to each other as well as a brother that was the mirror image of Ara. Twins, if you will. The Empyreans granted their children gifts and long lives." Now there were three different visions in the fire, three different worlds.

The visions changed to Earth, to ancient times moving slowly forward to the present. "As Gaia changed and her children evolved past their original creations, their life became shorter while her true children barely aged and retained their powers." The visions of Gaia shuttered and faded, in its place were two visions. One was of Ara. "The children of Ara and her brother Jaru retained their long lives. In each world a royal family was chosen, one that would become the voice for their Empyrean." On Ara she saw Grint, Lizbet, and an older woman who resembled Lizbet. Only possibility was that it was her mother.

"On Ara, the royal family was led by the male, who was the protector of Ara, while the females of the family were the mystics who would speak with Ara, giving out warnings of any danger and even seeing into the future if Ara granted. On Jaru, the roles would be reversed with the females of the royal family being the protectors while the males were the mystics." The visions changed and she saw a different world that resembled what she had seen here on Ara, except that instead of pastel hues the colors were more striking and bolder. The family were as Grint said, a woman standing proud in protector gear while the male wore robes that matched the colors of his world as did the son who stood before them.

"Jaru was the first to warn of the Ancients, not in time to save him, unfortunately." In the vision they saw the Ancients, in their silver refinery draining all the children of Jaru they touched. The bold colors of the foliage and terrain faded until only empty husks remained. A growl from behind her told her that the brothers were just as upset as she at what they saw. "The Ancients drained Jaru's children and depleted his resources, his essence. They took several of his children as their slaves, including the mystic."

The flames flickered while the images within changed, there stood a male in dark robes with silver accents. His short dark hair tight to his skull with dark eyes that felt as if they were staring right into you. Calista squirmed in her seat, her legs swinging off the bench onto the ground.

"The Ancients used the mystic of Jaru in many of their battles; the mystic led them to many victories, although he kept them from Ara. No one knows whether this was intentional, during this time Ara kept her children close and away from the Ancients. Our mystics, who had previously communicated through the stars, no longer were able to speak to one another."

The images shimmered and there in the flames were the Criptines that Calista had seen during the final battle in Atlantis. Beings of light whom the Ancients were unable to drain. "Jaru's mystic sent the Ancients to the planet of the Criptines where their numbers had been depleted, in retribution the ancients drained him. They did this before the other Champions in warning to any that wanted to betray them. Before his death, the mystic was able to get a warning to Ara that the Ancients were going to come for our mystic." This time the vision showed Lizbet in her robes.

"Through Ara, our Lizbet saw that the only way to defeat the Ancients for good was on Gaia." Images of ancient times on Gaia showed in the flames, the mortals living under the Gods and Goddesses rule in Greece, Egypt and even Scandinavia. "A prophecy that was unexpected was foretold to us. While Jaru and Ara's children stayed connected to their Empyrean, the children of Gaia had separated their lives from theirs. There was no mystic of Gaia as the children believed they were the true rulers of Gaia, whom they would eventually come to call Earth. To discover that a child of Gaia was the one who was going to save us all, had many of us perplexed but we knew better than to doubt our Empyrean."

The Ancients showed in the flames as Grint continued in his story. "The Ancients hadn't been completely decimated in the war with the Criptines, but their numbers had been greatly reduced and they were now on the run. The queen of the Ancients was now in hiding, her Ancients looking for a way to defeat the Criptines while avoiding them. They came to Ara, to take our mystic in their battle with the Criptines. It was here, on Ara, that our great hunter convinced the Ancients he could help them find the only one that could help them in their battle."

Calista frowned as the flames changed colors showing images of Ancients with their Champions standing there in front of Grint, Lizbet, Solen and the rest of the people of Ara. "The Ancients had a Champion who could tell if someone was lying, and it was this Champion who told them that Solen was telling the truth. And that was when the prophecy was set in motion." The images then showed the Ancients on different planets with different terrains standing before the people of the planet. "The Ancients gathered more Champions in their journey that they used as protection from the Criptines, looking for the one who would help them in their battle. On Gaia they found a seer who was coerced into helping them in their battle, her role in the prophecy had been written long ago." There in the flames Calista saw home, Atlantis. Although this Atlantis wasn't under the sea, the land was bathed in the sun. This was before the ultimate betrayal that sank her home to the bottom of the sea. Brax stood there next to a dark-haired woman who looked like an older version of Shaylane.

"When Brax's wife was taken." Calista breathed as she watched Trelaine leave with the Ancients. She saw other battles on different planets, some that ended with the Ancients leaving with other Champions, and then other battles that seemed to be interrupted by the Ancients that appeared. In one battle, they saw a Champion take down one of the Criptines. "One of the Ancient's Champions managed to capture the Criptine Princess, another part of the great prophecy."

The images that Calista saw showed the day that her home was cursed, showed Alastor kidnapping her from her crib before handing her to Ares and then imprisoning Aesis. She saw Solen, Draken, Rykar and her father there under the water. Solen reached for her hand, their fingers linked together as she just stared.

"And now that prophecy has come full circle." Grint turned to look at Calista. "Now, we have the one who will rid the universe of the Ancients." He held out his arms toward Calista and grinned. "Now, the end of the Ancients is near."

Calista felt as if they had just shined a spotlight right on her, she could feel everyone turning to look at her. Solen squeezed her hand in a comforting manner, she could hear Draken softly give a grumble growl, this version of him wasn't happy but he is willing to wait before going full dragon. She couldn't see Rikar but she knew that he was silently watching, nothing on the outside to show his irritation but every fiber of his being completely on alert.

Grint's arms fell to his side. "Let us feast upon the wonderful meal that has been prepared for us as we celebrate the coming defeat of the Ancients."

Standing up, she turned to look at the brothers and she could see that Draken was practically glaring at Grint while everyone around him cheered. She opened her mouth to tell him he wasn't starting anything here, not in front of Solen's family that she hadn't met yet. Just as she opened her mouth, she felt the air around her move. She was no longer standing but sitting next to Solen, whose hand grasped hers and squeezed just as he had moments before. Not only that but Draken gave another soft grumble. What just happened?

"Let us feast upon the wonderful meal that has been prepared for us as we celebrate the coming destruction of the Ancients." The cheers erupted around them as Calista sat there with Solen trying to figure out what had happened. She glanced around her to see if anyone was paying her any particular attention, but everyone's eyes were on Grint as they applauded. People started to move from their seats as she realized what she had been about to do before someone cast some sort of voodoo on her. She turned to find Draken but he was gone.

"You okay, Spider?" Solen was looking down at her.

"I think so." Her words sounded distracted as she looked around them. Rikar was smiling at a very disinterested looking Livinia, Kaine was chatting with a blond-haired woman who barely reached his shoulder but there was no Draken. "Yeah." She gave a small smile looking up at him.

"Good." Solen wrapped an arm around her shoulders. "How about we get some food and I will introduce you to my family and friends."

"I'd like that." Smiling up at him, she let him lead her away.

CHAPTER 10

The food was different from the food back on Earth, different texture, colors, and especially flavors. Calista and Solen were seated with Kaine and his family. Kaine's sister had a fair complexion with blonde hair while his parents shared his dark looks. Solen's family was seated with them as well; his little brother who had recently been accepted into the protection corps was a miniature version of Solen.

The bright green crystal looking shards that Calista tentatively bit into exploded into a flavorful burst in her mouth. Her eyes widened as she looked at Solen who was grinning at her while he chewed on his purple leaves. Swallowing he tilted his head watching her. "Not what you expected, was it?"

"No," she agreed looking at the multi-colored food in front of them. "Weird looking but more flavorful than any of the food back home."

"Think you might want to call Ara home?" Solen's words froze her in place, a purple leaf held between her thumb and forefinger merely inches from her mouth.

"Are you asking what I think you're asking?" Calista

felt as if her heart had stopped, as if time around them had slowed to a snail's crawl. Could she really stay here with Solen, on Ara where the people are so in tuned to their mother planet that they can actually talk to her? Looking around her at the people who seemed to be moving in slow motion, unaware of the internal discussion she was having with herself. This world felt more welcoming to her than Earth where the people destroyed their mother planet for their own comforts, soiled her water, soil and air in the name of progress.

So lost in her thoughts, her mind on the scenery around her, she didn't notice Kaine's little sister walking by her until it was too late.

"Ahhhh!" Calista jumped out of her seat, looking down at the blue, purple and green slime that was dripping down her front.

"Brooke!" Solen frowned at Kaine's sister who looked at him with wide eyes, although Calista was sure there was a pleased gleam in her eyes when she looked at the mess that was all over Calista.

"I'm sorry, I was just taking my tray to be cleansed in the fire and I tripped." Her bottom lip seemed to quiver slightly.

"That's all-right Brookey." Allen, Solen's younger brother, jumped up from his seat to comfort Brooke whose eyes lit up as he neared her. "Solen can help his guest and I'll make sure you get your tray to the fire with no more accidents." Allen winked down at Brooke who seemed to have already forgotten Calista and the so-called accident.

"Thank you, Allen." Brooke's smile seemed to light up. "I would really like that." She looked over at Calista, her smile slipping slightly. "I'm really sorry." Calista could hear the sincerity in her voice, which didn't match the look of satisfaction from earlier.

"You need help, princess?"

Calista looked over to see Rikar rising from his seat next to a very agitated looking Livinia. Draken's face was dark and scowling. She threw a reassuring smile their way. "I'm good, just going to change." She sighed looking down with a grimace.

Solen stood up with both their trays. "Let's cleanse these trays and then I'll find you a change of clothes."

She smiled gratefully as she followed him to the fire where he placed the trays completely in the fire before turning to grin at her, holding out his hand. "I think my mom has some clothes you can wear."

Calista looked at the purplish-blue pantsuit that Solen's mother loaned her. Short sleeves with a V neckline, side cut outs that show off her phoenix tattoo, accented with bluish boots since her white sneakers was another casualty from Brooke's food tray. A whistle from behind had her twirling to see Solen standing there with a grin.

"Looks much better on you than my mom," he grinned then frowned as his gaze moved down. "Now, that's new."

Calista looked down unsure of what he was talking about, then she saw her tattoo and understood. She gave a small shrug. "I had been waiting for you to come back for so long, when I was finally able to let go, it felt like I had finally started living again. So, to celebrate the new me, I got inked with a phoenix tattoo. A symbol of rebirth and new beginnings so to speak."

"Spider, I'm so so—"

Calista held up a hand to cut him off. "No, don't apologize. You had your war to fight, I understand that. You can't choose one person's happiness over thousands of lives."

He moved closer to her, his hands moving to hold her arms gently. "I wanted to, I wanted to leave and go back to you so many times. I wanted to end this war so we could be together."

"Except, if what Grint's little story said was true, you couldn't finish the war without me." She looked up at him.

He sighed.

"Did you know all that?" she asked, not understanding why he wouldn't have taken her when she asked to go, if he knew that.

"No." He gave a slow shake of his head. "Ara told our mystic what I must do when the Ancients arrived."

"Lizbet?" Calista asked.

"Lizbet." Solen nodded. "So, I told them what they wanted to hear, that I would help them in their battle with the Criptines but only if they would leave Ara in peace."

"And you believed them?"

He looked down at her tattoo, pausing before he responded. "Yeah, well, I'm a good soldier. Always do what I must to protect those that I love." She could hear the self-derision in his voice although she wasn't sure she understood it.

"So, you left because the planet told you to?" She wasn't sure how she felt about that.

"If I would've stayed, they would've taken Lizbet; she wasn't strong enough to handle that." His gaze wandered towards the open window where they could hear voices from outside. "Not to mention what would've happened to the others."

"Could Lizbet feel guilty about you leaving to save her?" Calista asked him, wondering if that could be the explanation of her behavior.

"I don't think so." He looked back at her, his lip curled up in that smile of his that she had so missed. "It was foretold that I was to be the one to find you but what no one saw was how hard I would end up falling for you."

"So, if I decided to go back to Gaia after we defeat the Ancients, you would go with?" She held her breath waiting for his answer.

"Haven't you figured it out? Where you are is home to me, Spider."

His words warmed her inside, made her want for the future rather than just living in the moment. A future with the man she loves and maybe even a child who could grow up with Draken's son. A family of her own. "You sure Ara didn't know about us in her prophecy?" Never having the gift of sight, she couldn't truly understand it. It just seemed odd to see into the future but yet not see everything.

"Prophecies are never absolute, nor are they completely accurate. The prophecy sent me to Gaia where it is said that the Ancients would be defeated."

"Which happened." Solen nodded in agreement with her words. "How often has Grint told that story?"

"You mean the one he told tonight?" It was Calista's turn to nod. "That was the first time we heard it."

"I thought he told the stories nightly? At least that is what I heard Allen and your parents talking about."

"Ahhhh." Solen breathed in understanding. "Grint tells the story Ara wants him to tell. Sometimes they are duplicates but not always. None of us had heard this one before tonight."

Calista nodded, looking back down at her borrowed clothes. "Does anyone here wear bold colors?" She looked back up at him. He raised a brow before looking down at his dark pants, boots and long jacket over his white shirt. She laughed. "So, you're the black sheep of the family then?"

"I guess I am." He chuckled, then held out his hand. "Walk with me?" She nodded, placing her hand in his.

Walking from his parent's home through the town still holding hands, Calista looked around them. They walked around the fire, Solen nodded in greetings to several of the townsfolk they passed. Childish laughter caught her attention, when she looked over to her left she saw Draken laughing and playing with some children who were running around him. It was good to see him smiling again, she missed that. She missed when both he and Rikar would tease her, even as they irritated the Hades out of her.

Speaking of Rikar, where was he? Looking around it took her a few minutes but she found him off to the side still in a romantic pursuit of the dark Livinia, who by the droll looks she was giving him, wasn't buying into his charm. That poor dragon, he had no idea how to handle rejection. She wasn't sure if she felt sorry for him, or felt he was getting his just desserts. After all, the broken hearts he had left back home could fill all of Ara.

"Livinia is something else, isn't she?" Calista mused as Solen wrapped an arm around her waist, lifting her up and over one of the benches that were situated around the fire. Her attention wasn't on where she was going, if not for his quick thinking she would've ended up on her face. She gave a bashful smile, pushing a lock of hair behind her ear. "Thanks."

"Not letting anything happen to you, not when I

just got you back." Giving her a wink, he looked over at Livinia. "She can be pretty scary, good thing she is on our side. It was during our last battle with the Ancients that we found her." He looked back at her. "The funny part was that we were there to save her and the other Champions, yet if it hadn't been for her, I can't for sure say that we would've been able to get out of there."

"Then I owe her my gratitude." Calista gave his arm a small squeeze as they kept walking. Ara was a beautiful place; the magic was everywhere. She could imagine living here with Solen, although there were a few things that would need to be discussed, she thought as she saw Lizbet sidestepping Livinia to speak softly to Brooke who was nervously biting her lip. But not now; now was just her and Solen.

"Tap, tap, tap, boom!" she sang as they walked, her fingers running over some flowers that reached out to her. As soon as the flowers touched her fingers, she could feel the Aggie within singing with her. "Tap, tap, tap, boom!"

"What is that?" Solen craned his head to look at her. "What are you singing? I don't think I've heard that before."

She laughed. "'Nuclear Reaction'."

"What?"

She laughed even harder at his expression. "'Nuclear Reaction' is one of Eon's favorite songs."

"Eon?"

She tilted her head, looking up at him. "Do I detect some jealousy in your voice, pirate?"

He leaned down until his nose touched hers. "Is there a reason for this pirate to be jealous?"

Moving her chin up she kissed his lips before laughing. "No, he's my little brother."

Solen backed up, eyes wide. "You have a little brother?" He asked incredulously as she nodded, amused by his reaction. "Wow, Cael and Malis had another child. And I missed it." He sounded so forlorn she squeezed his arm.

"You'll meet him when we go back to Atlantis to herald our victory," she told him.

"Tell me about him."

"Well, he's only a couple hundred years old but yet looks like a child." She grinned at his look of consternation. "By his choice."

"Why?" They were walking around the outskirts of town, Calista could hear the muted conversations in town as well as feel the presence of the Aggies all around them.

"No one really knows. Eon is different. While my grandfather is the herald of time and technology of old, Eon is his younger version in all. He is the God of new age, time and technology. No one knows if that is why he chooses to remain young and he has never said so." Calista looked around her at the beauty. "He would love to see this."

"He sounds interesting." Solen grinned. "I can't wait to meet him."

"He idolizes Draken."

Solen paused, looking over at her. "Now I really need to meet him, poor kid doesn't know that he is idolizing the wrong guy."

"Oh really?" She laughed, stopping when she felt a disturbance in the air around them. They both went into defensive positions as the plants around them started to glow. As soon as the stillness in the air came, it was gone. She looked over at Solen. "Is that normal?"

He shook his head and said, "No," as he looked around them with narrowed eyes. "I think it's time to get back to town."

She nodded, walking with him as she looked around. The stillness felt so familiar, although she wasn't entirely sure why. The glowing plants were dimming the closer they got to town. This definitely wasn't home.

CHAPTER 11

It had been several days since they landed on Ara, for the most part they were welcomed by everyone. Calista had spent some time in the forest with the Aggies, Bastion would stay by her side during each visit. Her and Solen had found out that they were the reason the plants were glowing, they said they were protecting them from an outside force but they didn't know from what or who. That sent chills down her spine, it also made it so that Solen told her not to leave town without an escort.

Draken had become more relaxed, even smiling with her. Rikar was still pursuing Livinia, something which was unusual. He struck out with each attempt to gain her favor, which wasn't something that had ever happened to him that she knew of. Could be good for him although she was surprised to see him still trying. She wondered what it was about Livinia that snared his interest, maybe they both could make a life here. Looking at Draken, she knew better. The brothers wouldn't be able to be that far from each other.

Calista would spend time with Solen's parents and

brother during the day, Allen would tell her stories about him and Solen when they were younger. How they loved anything that had their heart racing and the hairs on their arms standing on end.

"Or adding wrinkles to their poor mother." Their mother, Sylla, had interjected. Allen's lips twisted and he truly tried to look repentant but that gleam in his eye gave him away. "Like the time you chased a cratchor through the forest into the ziptuck fields where the spores had you both unconscious for days."

Allen shrugged. "I was the impressionable younger brother following his older brother."

"Hey!" he protested when Solen shoved him onto the floor.

"Boys." Sylla frowned at them as they started to wrestle around. She looked at Calista and sighed. "No matter the age, they still wrestle around like children."

Solen gave her an offended look, while Allen used the distraction to tackle his brother. Sylla gave Calista an *I told you so* look while she just laughed at the pair. After they both settled down, Calista asked what a cratchor was. Sylla told her it was a small fuzzy type mammal with a hard back, then showed her a picture that resembled a cross between a teddy bear and turtle. Calista thought it was cute while Solen informed her it was a delicacy, to which she frowned at that idea.

Many times, Kaine and his family would come to visit while she was there, that was when she discovered that their mothers had been best friends from a young age. Brooke was Allen's constant companion, the attraction between those two was easy to see. Brooke had started to warm up to her, even stopping her from trying one of the berries on a bush in the forest. It was the size of a golf ball with multi-colored bumps on it.

"That's a jezzball berry," Brooke had told her.

"Jezzball?" Calista had looked from the berry to Brooke.

"We use them for coloring clothes, painting and even in certain medicines." Calista's eyes went wide at hearing that.

"A plant that you can't eat, that you use for coloring clothes, is used in medicines?" Calista looked suspicious at the jezzball.

Brooke had shrugged. "Mostly external medicine."

"So, what happens if someone accidently eats it? Would it make them sick?" She hoped that was all it did.

"It can but the most noticeable effect of the berry is that it changes the color of that person's skin." There was a gleam in Brooke's eyes that had Calista curious. "Kaine was green for a whole week once."

Calista really wished she had seen that. "Why did he eat the berries? Was it when he was too young to know?"

Brooke snickered. "I didn't say he ate it on purpose."

Now the gleam was starting to make sense. "You little prankster." Calista giggled.

"Prankster?" Brooke frowned at her.

"It means playing jokes on others, like turning your brother green." It was as if the incident with the food spill had never happened. They could chat, joke and be at ease with each other.

Brooke gave a shrug. "I call it keeping everyone on their toes."

Calista laughed. "Fair enough."

That had been the day before; Calista was now chilling in the warmth of Ara's sun in Solen's mother's garden. Just like all of Ara, it was full of pastel hues. This garden overlooked the whole town, she could sit in a cloth type of lounger and people watch without being noticed which meant no socializing, which she liked. Back home in Georgia people watching was her way of relaxing, so many different people.

There were many people milling around the team, many residents of Ara that Solen had introduced her to in the past couple days, Champions that she remembered like Clori, Vlan and a few others that looked familiar but she hadn't been properly introduced to. Then there were a few she had never met like the two that seemed as close as brothers. One was bald, muscular with a hard look about him. She had only seen him smile once, so slight that she almost wondered if she imagined it. His companion was slightly smaller than him which wasn't that big of a feat since most was. Big and bald was rarely seen without Junior as Calista had come to call them both, not to their face but to herself.

Allen had told her that they were true adventurers. They would be the first to sign up for a mission and always be the first into battle. Although right now they were chatting with Draken, Rikar, Solen and Kaine. No Livinia in sight, she wondered if Rikar had given up or if Livinia had just managed to ditch him. She doubted either, Rikar was probably just giving her breathing space before his next pursuit.

Draken had even clasped Solen's shoulder in friendship like when Calista first came to Atlantis, a sight that gave her warm feelings. Draken had threatened Solen with dismemberment if he hurt Calista again, Rikar backing that threat up as well. After that, Solen's fractured friendship with the brothers seemed to have repaired itself. A good thing, when they got home she didn't want any tension within her family. At that moment she had also decided that it was time to spend some time with Kimi and Calton. Calton needed to get to know his Aunt Calista, and know that he could always depend on her.

She stretched her arms above her head, enjoying the warmth of the sun all around her. The day was coming to an end, she knew that she needed to get off the lounger and ready for the festivities that night. Solen had told her that they were having a celebration in her honor, first night a story in her honor and now this. She was ready for home where she was just Calista, the guys at the station back in Georgia would tease her relentlessly if she told them this. Not that she ever told them anything about her life as a goddess, not that they would believe her. But they were always good for keeping her grounded. "Okay Calista, let's go get ready and just remember to smile."

Solen's mother had loaned Calista a pastel purplish dress with blue and pink hues swirled within the fabric. This time she was wearing leather sandals that fit as if they were created for her. Solen slipped a light silver wrap around her shoulder as they walked with his family and Kaine's to the fire where everyone was waiting and watching them approach. Lizbet was standing with her father not looking their way, her lips pursed together and posture rigid. Tonight she would relax and enjoy the show but after tonight it was time Solen explained why Lizbet had a problem with them. It could be that she didn't like them because of how Gaia had been treated.

Although her father didn't seem to have the same hang up as he greeted them with a head nod. "I hope you enjoy tonight's entertainment; Velva is our most talented singer." He smiled at her.

"I'm sure I will." She hoped she sounded sincere, the urge to go back to her room in Solen's parents' place was riding her hard. With a deep breath she followed Solen and his family as they took their place on the bleachers in front of the fire where a silver shell was on a pedestal that was situated on a stage of sorts, right next to the fire. Solen's arm around her was comforting.

The light was waning around them as the sun was starting to set. The fire made it so that they would never truly be in the dark, also setting off an ambience as several people moved onto the stage. In their hands were instruments that looked almost celestial, shiny silver metal with crystal buttons. Some had long tubes while the others had circular openings and even strings. Then a female moved onto the stage, her long silver hair flowing behind her as if a veil. Her silk gown floated around her as she took her spot on the silver shell.

She gave a nod to Calista and spoke, her voice almost as perfect as she looked. "Tonight, we celebrate the defeat of the Ancients. The final battle is close,as is the end of the Ancients. Please enjoy my tribute to you." She nodded just a bit more. Calista just smiled, as she was unsure of what she should be doing. Thankfully, the music started as those with the instruments started playing and Velva started singing in soft melody.

"From under the sea to out in space,

Our warriors flee to win the race.

A battle they will fight,

A life they must save."

The air all around them lit up with sparkly lights and the foliage started to glow as they heard soft voices from all around join in harmony. She looked at Solen who was smiling down at her. "The Aggies are joining in; this is an honor that is rarely bestowed upon anyone." If she had any more honor bestowed upon her, she might not be able to withstand the weight.

"A life given.

A pain that burns.

A hazy vision.

A life returns."

Each sentence was spoken with more force than the previous melody. The lighted foliage flickered with the words.

"The final battle awaits,

A battle that will be fought alone.

No room for mistakes,

As the warriors enter the unknown."

Once again, the melodious tempo until the next verse repeated itself in the same force.

"A life given.

A pain that burns.

A hazy vision.

A life returns."

All lights dimmed, no flickers could be seen during the next verse as Velva's melodious voice sang a somber tone.

"In darkness the final war will be fought.

An ally will shake off his own death.

To avenge a past wrong that was wrought.

The war will be won with a last breath."

Calista's body went cold with those words, even Solen's arm lost its comfort.

"A life given.

A pain that burns.

A hazy vision.

A life returns."

With that final verse, the world around them was completely in the shadows, so silent Calista could hear her heart beating against her chest. It was as if the whole world of Ara had stopped breathing with the ending of the song. As the light around them started to grow brighter, everyone applauded. Even Calista, although hers felt empty to her.

Everyone was talking about the song and the music; the fact that the Aggies had joined was a big talking point. It seemed as if everyone who was talking about that was looking in her direction. But for once she wasn't paying that any mind, she was looking for Velva. She found her talking with Lizbet who seemed startled when Calista approached them. Calista paid her no mind this time, even when she found an excuse to leave.

"Velva, thank you for the concert." Calista smiled, reaching out to shake Velva's hand.

"You're most welcome, I was honored to be chosen," Velva told her, gently grasping Calista's hand in turn.

"Can you tell me how you came up with the words for the song?" Calista asked her. "What their meaning is?"

"I'm sorry, I wish I knew." The sincerity and compassion in Velva's face and voice backed her words.

"What do you mean?"

"I'm one of Ara's bards, I only sing what she tells me to sing."

Calista was unsure of what to say to that, so she nodded and turned to leave. Pausing, she saw several of the Aggies in the forest standing there, watching her. She moved forward to ask them about the words and their meanings.

"Calista!"

She turned to see Brooke running up to her with a smile.

"Time to go home."

She nodded to Brooke who nodded and rushed back to Solen, Kaine and the rest of the family. She saw Draken and Rikar standing with Solen, all of their faces solemn. She turned to look back at the forest but the Aggies were gone. With a sigh she moved to follow Brooke and the rest of the family.

CHAPTER 12

"A life given.
A pain that burns.
A hazy vision.
A life returns."

No matter how much she tried, Calista couldn't get that verse out of her head. A life given, it sounded so ominous. Yet the song was supposed to be an honor… some honor. It felt as if they were singing her obituary. Or at least someone's obituary, which wasn't any better. They had come to save Solen from himself and now it felt as if they had been pulled into another prophecy that they didn't ask for.

So much was happening it was hard for Calista to process it all. She hadn't thought much past getting to Solen. Now, she is part of another prophecy. She just wanted to help Solen free the Champions so he could come home with her and the brothers. Now, she wondered if they would even make it home.

"Sweetness, you haven't heard the best part yet." Rikar's cajoling voice pulled Calista from her dark musings. Turning towards his voice she came face to face with Livinia, her braids moving around her as if by their own will. Almost reminiscent of Medusa from back home, although there were no hissing snakes but actual hair. Livinia stared down at Calista, she wasn't that small but yet it felt as if most were taller than her. Where was the fairness in this?

"Your friend courts trouble." Livinia's voice sounded as dark as her skin.

Calista grimaced up at her with a shrug. "He always has."

"What are you two talking about?" Rikar joined them, looking between the two.

"Your imminent demise," an amused voice spoke. Calista turned to see Big and Bald with Junior standing there watching them. "Livinia isn't one to play around, unless it's with her prey."

"Vester. Vernon." Livinia nodded to each of them, her voice not hinting at any camaraderie or enmity. Calista was sure she had only had one tone as that was the only one she had heard from Livinia since their first encounter on the ship.

"Livinia." Each of the guys nodded towards her. Their voice, facial expressions and mannerisms expressed a kinship with one another. Livinia's gaze swept around and then she was gone as if she had never been there.

"Man, you guys scared her off." Rikar frowned at Vester and Vernon.

Big and Bald snorted. "No one scares Livinia off. If she leaves it's because she was either bored or not interested. I'm going to go with not interested."

"Are you guys friends of hers?" Calista moved so that she was between Rikar and them, Rikar had a pretty good sense of humor but even he had a limit. Thankfully he wasn't as hot headed as Draken, he seemed to satisfy himself with a glower in their direction.

"Nah." The shorter of the two shook his head. "No one is really her friend, but Vester and I were on the ship that rescued her and some others from the Ancients during Solen's last mission."

"So, you guys are Champions?" They nodded at her question. "What planet are you from?"

They looked at each other then back at her, their answer spoken in unison. "Here."

"Ara?" They nodded at her question.

"What? Did you think Solen was the only Champion they took from Ara?" She nodded at Vester's question, and he chuckled. "After Solen left with them those many years ago, they came back and demanded more Champions. They were going to take our sister but we persuaded them to take us instead."

"Sister?"

They both nodded. "You met her last night, Velva," Vernon told her.

"The singer." Calista looked at them, attempting to see the resemblance but honestly saw nothing. Vernon and Vester didn't even look related. Vernon had blonde hair that was just slightly shaggy with golden eyes and looked somewhat small standing next to Vester whose eyes were dark and as hard as his muscular physique. Three siblings that all looked completely different.

"She likes to be called a bard." Vernon grinned at her.

"Usually, her songs are more upbeat," Vester told her, his eyes full of sincerity.

"She sings what Ara tells her," Calista spoke, although a lump in her throat was making it hard. The brothers nodded but stayed silent, their compassion was written on their faces.

Rikar pulled her into his arms protectively and grinned down at her. "As if Draken or I will let anything happen to you, princess." She grinned appreciatively at him.

"Princess?" Vester and Vernon looked curious but she just groaned.

"Don't ask."

Vester's eyes twinkled as he opened his mouth, so she just shot him a dirty look and shimmered out before he could say whatever smart-ass remark that came to his bald head. What was it with guys and picking on her?

"Whatcha doing?"

Calista ended up on her ass on the ground with a

thud. She had thought if she stayed close to the forest that she might be able to find some alone time but it seemed that Brooke had found her.

"Sorry." Brooke truly seemed repentant.

Calista shook her head with a smile, standing up and dusting herself off. "No worries. What are you up to?"

"Heading to the joining ceremony of Robar and Anja. Saw you here and was wondering if you might want to come as well. They are holding it in Sala Way, one of the most celestial places on Ara."

"Sala Way? Sounds interesting." Calista wondered how it would compare to what she had already seen.

"Then you'll come?" Brooke gave an excited squeal when Calista nodded, bringing laughter from Calista. Brooke wasn't young in age but definitely young at heart and her excitement was infectious as Calista felt herself excited about the joining ceremony.

She let Brooke take her hand and pull her along the trail past the forest of the Aggies. "So, what is a joining ceremony?" She asked Brooke when she finally slowed down to a walk, letting go of her hand.

"According to Lissy a joining ceremony is equivalent to a wedding on Gaia," Brooke spoke as her arms were now swinging at her side while they walked.

Calista looked back towards the town where she was puzzled to see normal activity going on. "Are we the only ones going?" She looked back to Brooke, who was shaking her head.

"Not the only ones going, there will be some others from town there as well. Our joining ceremonies aren't as big as the weddings on Gaia, it is more for the couple than anything."

"Our weddings are about the couples," Calista protested, frowning at Brooke who just laughed.

"Yeah, but more about the couples being the center of attention."

"What's wrong with that? Won't Robar and Anja be the center of attention at this joining ceremony?" It sounded pretty hypocritical to her.

"In a joining ceremony, one of our divines will sit with the couple in the center of Ara where all four nations come together."

"Nations?" Calista tilted her head.

Brooke nodded. "On Ara, we are separated by nations and terrain but still together as children of Ara. We live in the Terrane nation where there is foliage all around and the Aggies protect our land. Then there is the Floe nation where it is bitter cold and the terrain is covered by ice and snow. They are protected by the Jinsons, creatures like our Aggies but they thrive in the colder environment. Ice blue skin, hands and feet padded with fur that had sharp claws for protection. They protect Ara and those who live within the Floe nation."

"Kind of like Inuits."

Brooke frowned at her words. "Inuits?"

"That is what we call those who live in the lands of ice and snow back on Ear..uh..Gaia."

"Oh, then … yeah, sure." Brooke continued. "Then the Pyre nation is covered in burnt fields with lava streams. Protected by the Karkens whose skin is as dark as Livinia's and eyes glowing brighter than the lava around them. Like the Aggies and Jinsons, the Karkens protect the ones living in their nation."

Calista's eyes widened at the images that flashed through her mind. "The people who live in the Pyre nation, are they just like you and I?" Brooke nodded. "How are they able to live in such an unforgiving environment?"

"That is all they have known, their physiologies have adapted to their terrain so that they can thrive there. While you and I wouldn't be able to, they do." Calista nodded although she was still having a hard time wrapping her mind around it. Brooke continued, "Finally, we have the Pura nation, which is covered in water, there are some terra there but mostly water with the aqua flora. Protected by the Carpes, who live in the water, they can breathe in water and on land. Their skin is a kaleidoscope of shiny blues, greens, golds and purples. The inhabitants of this nation have made their cities beneath the water, with the blessing of Ara they are able to breathe in the water as well as on land, just as the Carpes. The Aggies, Jinsons, Karkens, and the Carpes are Ara's Picknies. True children to her, they live within her. Some say when Ara speaks to her mystics, she does it through her Picknies."

"So, these other nations have mystics as well?" Calista looked around her in awe, thinking how there was so much more to this new world.

Brooke jumped up on a rock and did a forward flip landing on her feet before turning to look at Calista who had stopped and was watching her. "The people that live within these nations are our cousins, they don't look as we do but that matters not, we're still the same. Our nations rarely visit one another as the terrain and climate are so different. But when there is a joining ceremony, we rejoice and come together."

"Where?"

Brooke gave her a smile; one she wasn't sure she trusted. "You'll see."

Calista wasn't sure what she expected, if she even had any expectations, but even if she had, what she saw would've blown them all away with the sight of the water, ground, fire, and ice. Which is what she was looking at. Trees full of colorful leaves blossomed from a lava stream. Plants that looked like the coral of home in hues of blue, purple, and greens that adorned a glacier growing out from a mountainside with waterfalls emptying into colorful streams of ice. When they talk about a world where up is down and right is wrong, they must be talking about this place.

"Welcome to Sala Way." Brooke made a grand gesture, grinning at the look of wonderment on Calista's face as she looked around them. Brooke moved silently, but still with that big grin, towards where they saw a couple standing in the middle of a small pond of water. In that water was also an elderly gentleman in a gray robe with silver accents.

"They are in the pool of unity." Brooke spoke softly but clear enough that Calista heard her as they watched from a distance. "The one in the robe is our Purifier, he is one who determines if their unity is a true one."

"Purifier?" Calista frowned as she watched the robed male place his hands on the couple's head and slowly push them down into the water. She looked around where she could see others standing there watching, ones from the village and others from the different nations that Brooke had told her about.

"Yeah, he validifies the purity of the union." Brooke said watching as the water started to glow, the Purifier's hands still on top of the couple's head under the water.

"How does he know if the union is true or not?" As they watched the water seemed to shimmer and glow even brighter.

"All of Ara's children are born with a gift, one different from the one Ara bestows upon those who curry her favor such as Solen's ability as a hunter." Brooke started to tell her.

"Or Lizbet's mystical ability," she inputted.

"Eh." Brooke wrinkled her nose. "That one wasn't bestowed as it was more inherited. The gifts of Protectors and Mystics are inherited while others must earn their gifts." Her eyes widened as she realized what she had said. "Not to say our Protectors and Mystics didn't earn their gifts." She sighed but Calista just laughed.

"I got it." Turning back to the pond she was amazed to see that the couple were still under the glowing water.

"Anyways," Brooke continued. "The gift each of us is born with also helps us to find our true half. I'm not sure how to explain it except that this gift is meant for us to share a bit of ourselves with the one who is truly meant for us. The water is Ara's tears, they can see deep into your soul if you are truly connected to one another. If there is doubt in either of the couple, then the water would go dark with their deceit."

Something else occurred to Calista so she asked, "What happens if the union isn't a true one?"

A sigh could be heard from Brooke as they watched the couple rise from the water, shimmering as if the glowing water was still clinging to them. The looks of happiness on the faces of those in attendance was a sign the union was blessed. "If a couple attempts a joining ceremony that they know not to be true, Ara would punish them by taking away her gifts. All of them." Brooke bit her lip. "I know that's why Solen broke it off with Lizbet when he returned; he didn't want her to lose her gift or become an outcast for daring to betray Ara. I know it was hard on Lizbet, but I think after seeing you with Solen she finally understood why he had to do it." Brooke looked up at her with a smile. "It's plain to see the love you two have for each other." Brooke's smile turned into a frown. "Calista, are you okay? You look pale."

All around them trees started to shine, lava and glaciers glowed brightly as there were sounds of applause and happiness at the new union. Calista barely heard any of it, there was a roaring in her ears as her throat felt tight with barely contained emotion upon learning that Solen and Lizbet had at one time been a couple. Something that Solen could've told her but never did, but now she knew why Lizbet seemed so aloof with her.

CHAPTER 13

When they returned back to town, Brooke took off towards her brother who was talking with Lizbet. Lizbet turned slightly with a smile that faded when she saw Calista. Something Calista now understood. She fought down the impulse to confront Lizbet, she wasn't sure it would even make a difference. Besides, Lizbet wasn't the one who owed her an explanation, that would be Solen.

"Spider!"

She turned to see a smiling Solen running up to her, Rikar and Draken jogging up with him. She wasn't wanting an audience when she confronted him but at this point, she didn't care. She wasn't one to wait silently to speak her mind, she wanted answers and she wanted them now. "Why didn't you tell me that you and Lizbet were to be joined in a joining ceremony?" She was truly proud how controlled her voice was, considering how angry she was at him.

Solen was merely feet away from her when she spoke and he practically skidded to a halt. "Let's take this conversation somewhere private," he suggested as his eyes darted around them at the others standing there, attempting to look as if they weren't listening and failing.

"Why? My ignorance has been on display since I got here so why not have this discussion as well?" She asked him, her eyes glowing in her anger. Both Rikar and Draken had gone still behind Solen but she ignored them as her whole attention was on him.

"Spider…" Solen started but she interrupted him.

"Don't you Spider me!" Her hands clenched in fists at her sides, glowing as her voice raised. "Since arriving here I've asked you about Lizbet's behavior towards me, each time you've avoided answering me. I've been thinking maybe I did something to offend her and thinking what I could do to correct what I thought I did wrong."

"I'm sorry, I was trying to avoid conflict." Solen gave her a pleading look to understand but it fell flat with her.

"How's that going for you?"

"Not good at all." He gave a half grimace as he looked around at the small crowd that had given up on attempting to act like they weren't listening. Looking back at her he sighed. "I messed up, Spider. But I never meant to hurt you."

"So, why not tell me now?" Hands still clenched with power emanating from them, as if she wanted to strike at him, her glare cold as ice.

"Yes, me and Lizbet were to be joined before the Ancients came to this world. I gave up my freedom to save her from the Ancients. I directed the Ancients towards Gaia as was instructed, and started the prophecy that brought you into my life." Solen looked around them at the crowd that was now looking away from them, looking anywhere but their way. He looked back at her. "I was prophesied to bring you to Atlantis. What no one knew was how I would come to feel about you, I never expected that."

"Is Lizbet the reason you didn't want me to leave with you all those years ago?" Even as she asked the question, she wasn't sure she wanted the answer.

Solen shook his head. "I can truthfully answer, no," he told her. "I wasn't even thinking about her at that time." A strangled feminine pained gasp sounded from the crowd and the noise of someone running away from them could be heard. Calista was sure it was Lizbet and while part of her felt guilty, another part didn't care. "I truly am sorry I hurt you, Spider."

He moved towards her but she held up her hand. "No, I need to think… alone." With those words she did a sharp turn, running into his parents' house and the room she had been using since she arrived.

"Go away." Calista didn't even look to see who had entered her room after a brief knock before the door slid open.

"Nah, Solen and Draken are giving me a headache with their arguing."

She turned to see Rikar standing there in the doorway grinning at her. The fact that the two men that meant a lot to her were arguing would normally have her rushing to defuse the situation. This time she just shrugged. "Let them argue. Draken can be mad at someone else for once. At least Solen deserves it," she grumbled, tears slowly swelling in her eyes, leaning back in her chair.

Rikar, seeing her upset, attempted to comfort her. "Draken isn't always mad at you." He protested but at her snort he pressed his lips together and sat down on her bed. "Maybe Solen had his reasons."

"For deceiving me?" She turned to pin him with a look.

"I doubt he was trying to deceive you."

She sighed deeply, staring up at the ceiling attempting to gather her thoughts together before continuing. "I've had to deal with the jealousies of both yours and Draken's flavor of the week when I wasn't even in competition with them for most of our long lives." She turned her head to look at Rikar who was grimacing in response to the truth of her words. "Solen saw that when he was there, saw how uncomfortable it was for me and, no, the fact that it was a long time ago doesn't make it any better. To not tell me what was going on, letting me think I did something to offend her, was wrong. How can we stand the chance of being something stronger if he isn't honest with me?"

"Maybe he didn't want to ruin your time together," Rikar suggested.

"So, he lies?" She swung her feet around from her seat, setting them on the floor and staring at Rikar. "I'm sick of dealing with other's jealousies and insecurities that have nothing to do with me. Just because of their own insecurities they think it's okay to treat me badly, and treat me as if I were the bad guy? I'm tired of being the villain of someone else's made up story." Flopping back in the chair, she crossed her arms, furrowing her brow as she pursed her lips. She didn't care if she looked petulant, she had spent most of her life attempting to be the bigger person and was tired of it.

Rikar watched her silently for a few moments. Her frown deepened at his silence, she really hated when Rikar did that. He would go silent and just watch her, his expression making her feel as if she was being un-reasonable. She knew whatever it was that he was about to say, she wouldn't like it and she was right. "I wish I could answer your questions, princess. I really do. Except, the only one who can do that is Solen, and you ran away from him."

She scowled at him while he just watched her with a straight-faced expression. Finally, her expression re-laxed as she sighed. "You're right. Damn you, I hate it when you're right." This time he did grin as he held out a hand to her, after a moment hesitation she took it and let him help her up.

"Just remember to make him squirm for a good hour or so before you forgive him." She laughed at that but her laughter faded when she noticed the colored plant on her dresser that wasn't there before. "What's wrong, princess?" Rikar turned frowning but seeing nothing that was out of the norm for him.

"That plant." She pointed towards the plant, it was the same plant from Solen's special place that he told her to be careful around. "We need to get out of here carefully." She reached out slowly to Rikar, intending to grab his arm and shimmer out. That was her intent but before she could grasp Rikar there was movement by the plant, the air seemed to move although she could see no one.

Before she could figure out what it was that she was seeing, the room filled with the spores from the plant. Within moments the room had gone black as she fell into oblivion.

Calista's eyelids felt heavy as lead as she attempted to open them, not something you would expect a goddess to feel. Rolling over, she frowned, feeling the hardness of metal beneath her. When her eyes opened, she saw a scowling Rikar leaning against the opposite wall looking over to his left. Groaning, she sat up, luckily Rikar rushed to her side as she felt her world shift causing her to grow dizzy and start to fall back.

"Take it easy, princess." He helped her to lay back against the wall, watching her closely. "You good?" When she nodded, he moved back to his position.

"Where are we?" Calista looked around, frowning at the silver metal walls around them. Then she saw an open doorway. No door, no bars, nothing that would suggest they couldn't move through it.

Her intent must have been written all over her face since Rikar shook his head at her. "Don't do it." She frowned at him while he just motioned to the angry red mark that still glowed on his cheek. "I attempted that too and got a nasty bite."

"Bite?" Calista's eyes went wide looking at the doorway.

Rikar shrugged. "Felt like a bite, but whatever is there, it won't let us pass through without giving a painful shock that will send you on your ass."

"Oh." Calista looked away from the doorway, deciding to forget about attempting to leave the room that way. But there was always another way. She let out a scream of pain when she tried to shimmer from the room, it felt as if several thousand volts of electricity streaked through her entire body that went rigid with agony.

Rikar leapt over to her, his hands holding her convulsing body, staring at her with sympathy. "Yeah, I tried that as well with the same reaction. You good?"

She gave a pained nod, breathing heavily as she

leaned her head back. "Sure." She breathed out, sitting herself up but still leaning against the wall behind her. Frowning down at the metal bands on her wrists she looked up at Rikar who gave a nod and held his up where she could see his bands as well. "Great."

"You really think I would go through the trouble of taking you guys without a means of suppressing your powers?" Looking towards the door they saw Livinia standing there, watching them.

"You?" Rikar roared leaping for the door as Calista shouted his name in warning, but it was too late as he was thrown back against the wall beside her, landing in a heap on the ground, groaning in pain. Calista placed a calming hand on his shoulder as he glared up at Livinia. "Why?"

"I was hired to transport goldie here to my employer." Her words were spoken in the same tone as always, no emotion, just factual. "You just got in the way." Rikar glared at her.

"Who are your employers?" Calista had a sinking feeling she wasn't going to like the answer.

She was right.

"The Ancients."

Rikar growled, leaping up from his position on the ground, looking as if he was going to make another attempt to get through that door. Livinia just watched, no expression on her face.

"Rikar!" Calista managed to grab his calf before

he could get past her, stopping him in mid leap. She turned towards Livinia. "Why would you work for the Ancients?" she asked.

Livinia just lifted a shoulder in a nonchalant manner. "They pay well."

"That's your reasoning? They pay well?" Rikar stared at her in disbelief but she was already moving away from the cell they were in. "And to think I was considering giving you the honor of possibly being with me, after you passed an extensive interview of course." He looked from Livinia, who had paused to look at him, then to Calista. "Hey! A guy has to have his standards." Calista raised a brow but said nothing and he continued, "But that's water under Atlantis now. After this, I can promise you that you won't get another shot."

Livinia's usually deadpan expression cracked ever so slightly as she looked at him before giving an uncaring gesture as she turned again, walking away from them. "I will do my best to recover from the loss."

CHAPTER 14

"So, you think they've realized we're gone yet?" Calista asked as she stared up at the ceiling in their cell, not really looking at anything. Rikar had managed to find out from Livinia that they were on her ship that had been hidden from everyone on Ara, heading towards the Ancients. When he tried to get her to explain how she managed to hide the ship, she broke off the conversation by abruptly turning and walking away. She wasn't one for small talk, no matter how much Rikar tried.

"Depends on if they are done arguing or if their arguing turned into an exchange of fists," Rikar mused, staring at the cuffs on his wrist intensely, as if he could remove them with his hard stare.

"They wouldn't!" Calista's head jerked towards him.

He only laughed, lifting his head up to look at her. "Of course they would. Two testosterone filled guys protecting a woman they both love, each from a different perspective? Oh yeah, I guarantee punches will be thrown and bruises will come."

"There's no reason for them to do that." Calista frowned at him, her head shaking, not understanding what he was implying. They had no reason to fight; Solen lied to her, she was the one who had a reason to be mad at him, not Draken.

"That comment only shows how blind you can be."

"Excuse me!" Her posture straightened in her displeasure at what he said. His grin just added to her aggravation.

"You two talk too much."

Calista looked up to see Livinia standing there watching them; her usually neutral expression had a tinge of curiosity to it.

"That's how you get to know people, you talk to them," Rikar told her, an edge to his words.

"Why would you want to get to know people? There is not any reason. You either take the job or you do not. If you take the job, you get paid and move on to the next one." With each movement, no matter how trivial it was, her braids would move ever so slightly.

"Don't you want to know who it is you're working for?"

Her gaze moved from Rikar to Calista. "Why would that matter? As long as they pay."

"They enslaved you once, what makes you think they won't again after your usefulness has run out?" Calista couldn't believe that someone could be so blasé about working for people such as the Ancients, especially after the fact they had enslaved her.

"The Ancients never enslaved me." Livinia looked

down on her as she spoke. "No one enslaves my people. I was hired to bring you to them."

"So, you were planted on that ship that Solen freed," Calista stared at Livinia as some of the puzzle pieces were starting to connect.

"And your lover boy took the bait," Livinia confirmed. "All I needed to do was wait for your arrival."

"How did you know I would come?" Calista asked her, rising from the floor.

Livinia opened her mouth to say something before closing it, seeming to change her mind.

"How?" Calista demanded again.

If it was possible for Livinia to feel pity, Calista was sure she saw it in her eyes, ever so briefly. But she still didn't answer the question. "I would suggest you two resign yourself to your fate, we should be there in a couple of days." she said instead.

"Where is there?" Rikar questioned her. "The Ancients' home world?"

"The Ancients no longer have a homeworld, only encampments on various meteors they inhabit for a brief time. That is where I will be taking you."

"Couple of days?" Livinia turned back to Calista at her question. "What makes you think that our friends won't be able to catch up to you before then?"

"I have been planning this for months; I would not have taken you if I did not know I could get away with it."

"What do you mean by that?" Rikar gave Livinia a hard look.

"Just know that there will be no rescue coming for you, at least not before I hand you over to the Ancients." Livinia turned and walked away, leaving them both staring after her.

A whirring sound was the only warning they had before the wall opened up and bowls of colorful leaves with plates that had pieces of the colored meat they had eaten on Ara.

"At least she got the good food from Ara." Rikar took a bite out of the colored meat while Calista munched on the sweet leaves silently. Rikar watched her as they ate, placing his empty dishes back on the tray. "So, you going to forgive loverboy?"

Calista looked at her empty bowl and sighed, glancing up at him. "You seriously want to talk about that now?"

Rikar snorted. "What else are we going to be doing? We're sitting in a cell that we can't get out of, in a ship that even the gods don't know where it is, unless you have something more interesting to talk about." The expectant look he threw her way pulled a deep sigh from her.

"Fine." Her words were spoken through tight lips. "I'm sure I'll forgive him... eventually."

"Eventually?" Rikar raised a brow.

"What do you want me to say?" she asked him with a heavy breath.

"We don't know what is going to happen, if we'll even see them again but you say that you'll forgive him eventually?" She glared at him. "It was innocent jealousy."

"Innocent jealousy?" She raised her brows at him.

"Yes." He nodded. "When they first got together, he didn't even know about you."

"And?"

"And... he broke up with her rather than lead her on." Rikar shrugged. "Seems pretty innocent to me."

"If it was that innocent, he could've told me," she grumbled, flicking her nails.

"It has been centuries since he last saw you and you wanted his first words to be about another woman?" The sardonic question grated on her nerves. She hated it when he got serious, it was so much easier when he was playing around.

"He had several chances since then." she pointed out to him with pressed lips.

"I can't speak for him but if it was me, I would've rather spent the time talking about anything but another female."

She stuck her tongue out at him and flopped back with crossed arms. "I'm not liking you very much right now." His laughter bounded all around, she had to press her lips together to keep her smile from breaking. But the twinkle in his eye showed that he saw.

The ten foot by ten foot cell they were being held in was feeling cramped after who knew how many hours they had been there. Calista found her eyelids growing heavy. How she could become tired while in captivity was beyond her, but she was.

"Get some sleep." She looked over at Rikar who was watching her. "I'll watch over you."

She wanted to argue, after all, she was good at it. But she also wanted some sleep, it only took a few seconds for sleep to win. With a nod she let herself slump there against the wall, her eyes closing and a welcoming darkness taking her. At least this one was a willing one. From the fog of sleep she heard some conversation.

"So, where are your people from?" That was Rikar's voice.

"A planet in a solar system several light years away from here." That level toned voice was Livinia. She lifted her eye lids just a bit, enough that she could see Rikar and Livinia through the slits.

She could see the tightening around Rikar's eyes that signified his irritation with Livinia's answer. Both him and Draken were used to women fawning over them, she never got to see the courting of Draken and Kimi to know if Kimi made Draken chase her but it looked as if Livinia was going to make Rikar chase. "Does this planet have a name or are you going to keep avoiding the question?"

"I am not avoiding any question; you did not ask the name of my planet."

"Well, then." Rikar's smooth voice showed his irritation. "Let me change the question, Miss Literal, what's the name of your planet?"

"Baling."

Rikar nodded. "How did the Ancients hire you if your planet isn't in this solar system? Look you up in the want ads?"

"Want ads?" She frowned.

"Yeah, put out an ad in a newspaper looking for a local kidnapper who can pretend to be a friend." The sarcasm was very evident, although Livinia either couldn't hear it or just completely ignored it.

"No, our people are well known for our unique abilities. Many seek us out." While her words sounded full of conceit, there was none in her tone.

"Unique abilities?"

"My people are the best assassins or, as Lissy says, guns for hire. I believe that is a phrase used from your home world."

"Assassins? As in killing?" Rikar's voice took on an edge.

"Yes, if that is what is required." There goes that

literalness that Rikar teased only moments before. Livinia didn't seem to hear the edge in Rikar's voice that meant he was on the defensive, but Calista did. She could also see how taut his features and posture had become at those words. "My people have a code and that code is our contract. We live and die by that code, we never break a contract, that would be like signing our own death sentence."

"What do you mean by that?" Rikar was still tense, although his curiosity was winning. Calista was feeling the same curiosity, she was also sure that he was attempting to find out more about their captor and hopefully a way to secure their freedom.

"If any of my people were to break a contract, one of two things will happen, depending on the severity of that breach."

"And those are?"

Livinia watched him closely from her position by the door for a few seconds before responding, "Either executioners are sent after the defector, or worse, they are banished from our home world."

"How could banishing be worse?" Calista shared Rikar's confusion on that.

"We are a solitary race, taught to rely only on one's self. We have no need or desire for closeness of any kind."

"Still not understanding." Rikar frowned at her.

"To achieve the balance that one needs to survive in

such single solidarity, my people need to reset oneself after each mission in the Halls of Divided Union."

"You do realize that those two words do not go together."

Her brow furrowed just a bit at his words. "Why not?"

"Division and union aren't the same thing; they have no common ground."

"I disagree."

"Really?"

"Yes, to be able to work in solidarity but yet as a unit, our people need to be able to know how to separate ourselves and yet, at the same time, work together."

"How do you guys get anything done? That sounds like a complete oxymoron." Rikar looked just as confused as Calista felt, she almost failed in keeping up her appearance of being asleep due to being stunned by Livinia's comments.

"Oxymoron?" Livinia frowned at him.

"Yeah, two things that don't go together. Like handsome and ugly, they are oxymorons of each other." Rikar sighed, Calista could tell that his words weren't getting through to Livinia. His look went from aggravated to pensive, she was curious what plan was forming in that devious mind of his. Hopefully one that would get them out of this predicament. "You say that you take contracts?"

"Yes." Livinia nodded.

"What if I were to offer you a counter contract?" Livinia looked at him silently, as if waiting for him to elaborate. "What if I wanted to hire you?"

"And what would you hire me for?" Livinia actually seemed to enjoy this banter with Rikar, it wasn't due to any expression since she barely had any, but the fact that she hadn't walked away yet. Calista was sure this was the longest she had stayed anywhere for any conversation.

"To escort me and the princess of Atlantis back to Ara."

"And the payment?" Livinia's head tilted ever so slightly, giving Calista a small slimmer of hope that Rikar's charm was actually working.

Rikar stood up, leaning against the wall by the doorway watching Livinia. "You take us back to Solen on his world and when we get back to Gaia I will show you my cave with all my valuables. You can bathe in diamonds while wearing a topaz crown." He even threw in one of his boyish grins that was a fan favorite back home.

Her lips twitched, almost amused. "Diamonds and topaz might be valuable on Earth, but not out here."

"Then what is valuable to you?" Rikar countered.

"It matters not." Her tone had gone back to the dismissive firm tone of earlier. "I cannot take a new assignment without finishing the current one."

"So, you're just going to deliver us to the Ancients without even considering my proposal?" Rikar and

Livinia were both staring at each other. Calista was wondering who would look away first.

"Her?" Livinia nodded her head towards Calista, although her gaze still trained on Rikar's face. "Yes. She was the one I was contracted to bring to them."

"What about me?"

"Your name is not on the contract, after I drop her off, I will send you back to the others." Livinia spoke as if that would be just like driving up to the planet and letting him out of the ship. How did she think it would be that easy?

"You think I'll allow that?" Rikar frowned at her. "That I would allow you to hand her over to the Ancients while I traveled with you back to Ara as if nothing had happened?"

"You do not have much choice."

The clenching of Rikar's jaw was a sign how her words upset him, it was hard for Calista to keep pretending to be asleep but she had a feeling that if she "woke" up that the conversation would end. She wanted to listen, after all it was her life as well that was hanging on Rikar's ability to flirt. She saw his face relax as he seemed to realize something, he licked his lips before asking, "So, you're not going to kill me then?"

"I was not hired to kill you."

Rikar gave a patronizing nod with a smirk. "You sure that's the reason?"

This seemed to actually give Livinia pause as her brow furrowed just a bit. "What do you mean?"

Rikar leaned closer to the doorway, his eyes crinkling with his smile. "I had a feeling I was wearing you down these past few days. It's okay to admit that you have feelings for me. How could you not?"

Calista barely stifled the groan, one of Livinia's dark brows slightly twitching was the only sign that she was affected by his candor as she responded, "We will be at our destination within the day. If I were you, I would spend as much time as you can with your friend." With those words she was gone.

"Yeah, she has it bad." Rikar nodded and grinned.

"What? Constipation?" Calista sat up, her head tilted back so she could see the faux shocked look he gave.

"Princess!" His disapproving tone reprimanded her for saying such a thing.

She grimaced. "I wish you would quit calling me that."

"Stop running from it and maybe I will." He stayed in his spot against the wall.

"Nothing to run from," she told him, barely stifling a yawn.

"You're the granddaughter to the rulers of Atlantis, what does that make you?" he countered.

"Lucky?"

"Argumentative."

Her laughter bounced off the walls of their cell. "Whichever works."

CHAPTER 15

It is time." Livinia was standing there at the doorway staring at them. "Let us go."

Rikar, who had already been standing, moved towards the open doorway, tentatively reaching out his hand. When there was no bite, he moved through the doorway. Before he could get close to Livinia she held up a small black box.

"I would not attempt anything unless you want to be on the ground writhing in pain," she warned him.

Rikar glared at her before turning around to help Calista up, making sure he was positioned close to her. She knew he hated not being able to protect her. Hell, she hated being defenseless, but not much either of them could do about it.

"Solen took you in and treated you like a friend." Calista spoke up as they moved through Livinia's ship. "You betrayed that friendship; how could you?"

"It is nothing personal, just a job. The Ancients knew what ship your hero was going to hit so they knew where to place me. They made sure that he was able to rescue everyone."

Calista stared at her in horror. "So, they sacrificed

their own people so that you would be rescued by Solen?"

Livinia nodded. "As I told you before, I was paid to go with Solen to wait for you. Then I was to take you to them any way possible." Livinia moved flawlessly through her ship, leaving Calista and Rikar to do their best to keep up as the bands on their wrists made sure they kept following her.

"What are you going to do when the Ancients turn on you?" Rikar asked her as they followed.

"I am here to drop you off, collect and then leave. There will be no time for them to turn on me." Livinia spoke easily as if she was giving them directions to the nearest gas station.

"You keep thinking that." Rikar glared at her back. "I hope I'm there to see you proven wrong."

Calista cringed at the venom in his voice, although she understood it. She felt betrayed as well. Solen probably wouldn't be too happy about it either, hopefully she would see him again. Right now, her anger at him seemed diminished when all she wanted was to feel his arms around her. "How did the Ancients know which ship it was that Solen was going to hit? How did you know that I would be coming there?" Calista asked, hoping she would get an answer this time.

Livinia paused, breathing in and then turning to look at them as they stopped behind her. Calista wanted to believe that she would finally answer her questions but she refused to get her hopes up. She was greatly surprised. "There is one in Solen's camp who happened to want you gone as much as the Ancients wanted you."

Calista stared at her, watching as Livinia turned slowly around and looked at her. As she stared into those dark eyes she knew, her body felt numb. "Lizbet?"

Livinia nodded, watching as Calista processed the information. "Lizbet told the Ancients which ship Solen was going to attack to make sure I would be on it. Then she made sure to get you to Ara, where I would be waiting. She told me of the plant that would help me get you to my ship with no problem, as long as I could avoid the toxin."

"How did you avoid the toxin?" Calista had to know.

Livinia gave a half shrug. "There is no toxin that can affect me or my people."

"Isn't that nice?"

Livinia nodded. "It is. It is also helpful in our work."

"I bet it is." Rikar grumbled.

Calista held up her wrist with the metal band. "Did she give you these as well?"

"No." Livinia shook her head. "Those were given by the Ancients to help suppress your powers." She looked over at Rikar. "They gave me two, just in case, and it looks like it was a good idea."

"Don't you have any feelings?" Rikar asked her.

Calista was sure she saw a twitch in Livinia's

expression at his question but her face had the same stoic features when she answered him. "Feelings get in the way, make you weak. That is not the way of my people, we are a strong race that is ruled by no one."

"Yeah, well, feelings make me stronger." Rikar told her.

"If you say so." She didn't look convinced.

"Take these off and let's find out." He invited but she ignored him, turning around and pulling them along once again.

"Let us go."

Calista looked over at Rikar as they moved along behind her. "Innocent jealousy?"

He gave a half grimace. "I've been known to be wrong a time or two, doesn't happen often but I can admit it when it does." At her glare he gave her one of his smiles that tended to make her give in. It wasn't the flirty look he gave all the ladies; this was the big brotherly one that always had her leaning in to get a big brother hug. Not that she was able to right now. "Sorry, princess."

"If we get out of this, you better believe you'll be making it up to me," she grumbled at him.

"When we get out of this, I will," he promised, putting emphasis on the when.

"Livinia." The term from back home about nails

on a chalkboard came to Calista's mind upon hearing that voice, the mediocre, monotone voice of one of the Ancients. How long had it been since she heard those voices? Not long enough.

Calista and Rikar had been so engrossed in their surroundings since leaving Livinia's ship, they hadn't seen the Ancients until they spoke. Checking out their surroundings as they walked, noting where they saw ships stationed on the off-chance they managed to escape. Taking stock of the different Champions that were stationed around this dystopian looking fortress of the Ancients that was carved into this flying rock of a meteor. One of the eerie things about this place was that when looking up, Calista could see the darkness of space but yet they were able to breathe and walk without floating into space. Which meant there was some sort of shield protecting this fortress.

Calista looked at the silver beings in front of them. Three of them, two males and one female all with that same inexpressive look they try to carry. Although she still remembered the looks of rage on the ones they fought back in Atlantis. Her fists clenched by her side as she stared into the silver faces that looked both her and Rikar over.

"And you brought us an extra gift." The lips on the female Ancient curved into a small smile. Rikar growled at her and the bands on his wrist glowed brightly, which had his body tensing in pain although he refused to let the pain bring him to his knees. A grunt was the only verbal acknowledgement of the pain. Calista was sure she saw a glint of satisfaction in the female's eyes, which had her pressing her lips together as she leveled a hard stare but said nothing.

"It was necessary for the moment; I will return him once our business here is finalized." Livinia told them.

"No need," the female told her dismissively, holding up a hand. The female Ancient moved closer to Rikar who was watching her movements. "We have a use for him."

"He was not part of the contract," Livinia countered.

"No worries, there will be some extra compensation in your payment," one of the males informed her.

She opened her mouth to possibly protest.

"Unless you want to join them, I would take your payment and leave." Calista could see the slight widening in Livinia's eyes at his words, then they narrowed but she gave a curt nod before turning and leaving. "Now then, let's show you to your accommodations." This male turned away, Livinia already forgotten, leaving Calista and Rikar to follow along helplessly. They had no choice, the Ancients were now in possession of the small remote that had the bracelets pulling them forward.

"We don't live the lavish lifestyle of our predecessors, but it does suit our purpose." The male spoke as they moved along towards a tall metal building ahead.

"Which is?" Calista asked, staring ahead as they followed them, but her eyes were looking all around, trying to take their surroundings in.

"Giving us a place of operations while we complete our best weapon of defense and making it operable." The mediocre tone belied the malevolence behind those words.

"And who are you?" Rikar spoke and the female paused in her stride, coming to a halt in front of them. Turning around to give Rikar another once over with a slight smile.

"Forgive us, being banished to the farthest reaches of this solar system has made us rusty on simple pleasantries. My name is Risa, my two companions are Ryno and Riso." Each male nodded when Risa said their names. They had different names than the ones that came to Atlantis and their features were slightly different but they still had the silver skin, clothes and eyes.

"Making it down the alphabet, are you?"

Risa stared at him. "Alphabet?"

Rikar lifted a shoulder. "When the Ancients came to Atlantis, some of their names were Lux, Loom, Lore and Lars. Seemed all their names started with an L, yours all starts with an R. Making it down the alphabet."

The narrowing of Risa's eyes was so slight, Calista wasn't sure that was what she was seeing. "We go by the name our Queen Mother gives us." That was all she said before turning to continue their way past another hangar where more ships were stationed. So, they had two hangars. "Our numbers have been greatly diminished, thanks to that traitor, Solen. You, of course, call him a hero."

Calista felt the sharp look that was thrown her way. "Afraid I can't drum up enough sympathy for your plight. You, who thrive off of other's pain, are getting your karma."

Ryno turned to look at her, not pausing in his stride. "Your sympathy is not wanted, nor is it needed. You'll be the key to our return to power, that's all that matters and the only reason you live now."

"I won't help you guys do anything." She kept walking, staring ahead and doing her best to memorize their journey. If they get out of this, she wants to know how to make it back to one of the hangars.

"You seem to mistakenly think you have a choice." Ryno returned.

"I would rather die than help you parasites out," Calista practically spat out. Ryno turned but Riso placed a placating hand on his shoulder.

It was Risa who responded, "I will put this as plainly as I can, so that your simple mind can comprehend your situation and you can forgo all these foolish thoughts of free will. You have no choice in helping us. We will use you in our rise to power, after your usefulness has been completed then your wish for death will be granted."

"Not while I breathe." Rikar growled, then grunted as the silver wrist bands glowed.

Ryno threw him a contemptuous look. "Who says you'll be breathing?"

"I definitely won't help if you hurt him." Calista glared at the silver robotic parasites who seemed to enjoy their distress.

Risa sighed. "If it makes you feel better thinking you have a choice, then by all means, feel free to continue your daydream."

"We must get ready for your friends who will surely come to your rescue," Ryno told them, looking at Rikar with a satisfied look. "That's where you'll come in handy."

"Like Hades I will." Calista could hear the frustration in Rikar's voice and wanted to scream out at the unfairness of it all. Neither of them asked for this but yet here they were.

Ryno just shrugged as they moved through hallways away from the hangar. "This ship is the main one in this fleet, the only one that was built into a meteor. We siphoned the energy from it to help us create ships and weapons for us and our Champions that are still loyal."

"This was a star?" Calista's eyes widened.

"Was being the key word," Ryno told her dismissively.

"You drained a star until it became a dead piece of rock floating in space?" She gave them horrified looks but none of them seemed fazed by her words.

Risa lifted her shoulders. "That is the way of life. We needed the energy to survive, the star had it, so we took it."

"We might not have as many fleets as before, but the ones we have are strategically placed so that they will be useful when needed," Ryno stated as they turned down a hallway into a circular room. All around them were open doorways to small square rooms that Calista could only assume were small cells. "Welcome to your lodging for the duration of your stay here." With a push of a button Calista felt herself pulled by the wristbands into the room. The open doorway lit up with energy before Rikar could enter. "Not you, not yet. Time for you to be useful."

"No!" Calista screamed, turning and moving as close to the doorway as she dared. "Leave him alone!" Her heart pounded in her chest so hard at the thought of what their term 'useful' meant.

"Don't worry princess, I'll be okay." Rikar attempted to comfort her.

"Keep telling yourself that." Ryno smirked, pushing a button on the remote which compelled Rikar out of the room while Calista shouted at them to return him.

CHAPTER 16

Calista wasn't sure how long Rikar had been gone, she had heard his screams of pain echoing down the hallways for what felt like hours. Tears coursed down her face; her voice hoarse from screaming for them to bring Rikar back. Exhausted both mentally and physically, she was seated on the floor of yet another cell, leaning against the wall.

The sound of the energy barrier opening made her look up to see two Ancients she hadn't seen before, shoving Rikar into the cell and letting him fall. They had the same silver hair, skin and eyes but they were a bit more muscular. They left as the barrier lit back up in the doorway. Calista rushed to Rikar, her hand that had barely touched his shoulder drawing back at his groan of pain. "What have they done to you?"

"Be thankful." Calista looked up to see Risa standing there watching them. "We were afraid we would have to use you instead, which would've set back our timetable longer than we would have liked."

Calista moved to place Rikar's head on her lap, the bruises she saw around his temples, neck and shoulders brought tears to her eyes. She looked up at Risa. "Timetable for what? What is it that you guys want me for?"

"No worries, you'll find out soon enough." Risa watched Rikar groaning on the floor as Calista ran her hand along his sweat-dampened hair, pulling it from his face. "Your friend should be honored."

"Honored?" Calista couldn't stop the dumbfounded tone in her voice.

"Yes. Since Solen's return, Ara found a way to shield herself from any attack we could deliver. We've been working on a way to cut through her defenses with no luck until a year ago. One of our scientists managed to create a power cannon of sorts but no way to power it. We've tried using Champions who've fallen from favor but they didn't even give a blip of power before they expired completely." Calista sat there, holding onto Rikar as she listened to Risa speaking about basically killing someone with little to no emotion. "We had even attempted taking the power from a star but we had no way to make it compatible." She let out a small sigh. "We started to lose any hope that we would be successful."

"If you attacked Ara, you would've killed your little informant there as well," Calista shot back at her but Risa only shrugged.

"As long as she has served her purpose, we've no more need of her."

Calista didn't have any warm feelings for Lizbet, she would love to knock the idiot on her ass but those words were spoken so coldly and exactly that it sent unwelcome shivers down her spine. "That is cold."

"That is the way of things."

Calista shook her head at Risa's words. "No, that may be your way of doing things but that is not the way of things for others. We care about life, value it."

"Then you are foolish." Risa's voice took a condescending tone as she sneered down at Calista. "So, we had finally created the ultimate weapon we needed but hadn't been able to locate a source powerful enough that could be adapted for our weapon." Her scornful gaze lighted upon Rikar. "Then Livinia gifted us with a spare. We were able to strip his power down to fuel our machine, if he lived through it then he might be of more use but if he didn't, then no matter." She shrugged with a malicious smile.

"I was wrong, you're not parasites," Calista said while shaking her head. Risa's head tilted with interest at her comment. "You're monsters."

Risa's eyes narrowed. "Your opinion matters not, Solen will pay for his betrayal and constant attacks against us. He's the reason that we're hiding out here in the farthest reaches on this forsaken piece of rock when we used to fly on magnificent ships with throngs of servants and Champions."

"You mean slaves," Calista countered.

Risa repeated, "It matters not, soon we'll be back to our former glory, and it will be thanks to you." With those words she turned and walked away, leaving Calista there holding onto Rikar who was staring forward with unseeing eyes.

Calista gently rocked while she held onto him as he lay there on her lap. "I'm so sorry." Her voice broke as she spoke to him. "If not for me, you wouldn't be here."

"Not your fault," Rikar told her in his weak voice, he attempted to push himself up but only succeeded in slumping back on her lap with a weakened growl. "Dammit, this sucks."

Calista gave a small smile, placing a calming hand on his shoulder. "Rest, dragon boy."

He gave a weak chuckle. "Been a long time since you've called me that."

"Been a long time since we've been together for this length of time," she said as her fingers smoothed his hair back.

"True." He nodded. "We really need to rectify that."

"We will," Calista told him. "Promise." She did her best to keep the tears at bay as she prayed that they would have the chance. She worried about them, she worried about Solen with everyone on Ara and she worried about their family back on Earth. If the Ancients succeed in whatever they were planning, she was sure that no one would be safe.

A sound outside the cell pulled Calista out of the stupor she sunk into while her and Rikar were left alone in their cell. There stood an Ancient although this one seemed different from the others. Not quite an adult but neither was it a child, more like an adolescent. Just standing there staring at them through the energy barrier, saying nothing.

"What do you want?" Calista asked, there was no malevolence in her voice, but neither was there any warmth.

"Wanted to see what you looked like." The Ancient spoke with the same monotone as the others, without the maturity. Barely four feet tall, hair that was slicked against the skull wearing a silver robe that wrapped around their torso and hung down to barely four inches from the floor. "The one who powered our mighty cannon and the one who is going to bring us back to glory."

It was on the tip of Calista's tongue to tell him she wasn't going to help them do anything but she knew it would be a waste of breath, so she just stayed silent. Rikar moved slowly and jerkily on her lap, attempting to push himself up. He almost succeeded. This time he at least managed to sit straight up before he slumped back into her lap. "You've seen us, now go away." He grumbled weakly at the Ancient who continued to stare.

"What happens when you attempt to attack Ara and your so-called weapon fails?" Calista queried the Ancient. "Then all on Ara will rise and destroy you."

154

"We wouldn't take such a foolhardy risk." Ryno appeared, looking down at the adolescent Ancient. "Ricci, go to your station, be ready." Ricci nodded up at him and left. Ryno looked back at Calista, with a superior look that she truly wanted to wipe from his face. "Before we head to Ara, we will have an opportunity to test the weapon to make sure it will do what we need."

"How?" Calista asked before she could stop herself, not that she could be sure of an answer.

"Your friends will be coming to your rescue." Ryno's lips curled viciously at the look of dread in her face. "We will have a surprise for them."

"No!" Calista breathed out as Ryno walked away with a satisfied look. "NO!" she screamed as Riker weakly growled, still unable to rise. She shook her head, her eyes burning from unshed tears that she was barely keeping contained. "We can't let that happen."

"We won't." This time Rikar was able to roll over and push himself up off the ground with shaking arms. "We will stop them."

"How?" Calista looked around them for anything that could help them.

"Getting out of this cell would be the first step." Both Calista and Rikar jerked their heads up to see Livinia standing there outside their cell.

"What are you doing here?" Rikar growled at her.

"Freeing you from captivity," Livinia told him. The energy barrier fading as she pushed a few buttons on the wall. "Now, we need to get out of here before they come back."

Rikar lunged at her but all he ended up doing was grabbing her arms as he slid to the ground in front of her. Calista moved quickly to help him up with Livinia's help. Looking at their dark-skinned savior Calista asked her, "Why?"

"Because I have lost what common sense I have." Livinia's answer confused Calista but Rikar gave a weak little chuckle.

"Couldn't leave me behind, could you?" Calista gave a silent groan at his arrogant response but he paid her no mind. "I knew I was wearing you down."

"You seem to be the one who is worn down," Livinia told him.

"Just give me a bit of time, I will bounce back." Rikar grinned.

"Did you take Rikar's counter offer?" Calista asked her as they both helped Rikar semi walk, semi crawl between them.

"You could say that." Was the vague response then she shrugged. "You could also say that no one alters a contract with my people."

"You want us to trust you, then maybe you should say more than that," Calista told her.

Livinia looked at her. "You want a reason to trust me?"

"It would be nice and go a long way to us working as a team."

"Fine," Livinia said, her braids flying towards both Calista and Rikar before either could move. Not that Rikar was in any shape to evade the hair projectiles. The braids snapped at the metal bracelets on their wrists, and with each crack the bracelet broke apart and would've fallen to the floor if not for those same braids that grabbed the pieces of metal and offered them to Calista. Calista pocketed both pieces. "Hopefully that will be enough to convince you so that we might get off this rock so you can warn your friends before they get here."

"For now," Calista told her. "Later, I'll want a more detailed answer."

Livinia nodded and they moved once more, this time in silence as they both tried to balance helping Rikar move forward while watching for any Ancients or Champions. A scuffle could be heard ahead of them in the parallel corridor. Calista looked over at Livinia who shrugged her shoulders but reached into her jacket and pulled out a lethal looking knife. Her braids were also weaving around her head as well, Calista had a feeling they were just as lethal as that knife.

"Whoa!"

Calista leapt into Draken's arms when they almost collided, so happy to see him. Draken held onto her, hugging her to him. "Cali, you're a sight for sore eyes." While Rikar had always refused to drop the princess, Draken had no problem dropping it. Although, it had been a long time since he called her Cali.

"Hey, how about letting me greet my Spider." Solen glared at Draken but Calista just smiled moving out of Draken's embrace. Her face lit up as she felt Solen's arms embrace her, something she had worried she would never feel again. He looked down at her. "We're supposed to be rescuing you, you know that right?"

Calista shrugged. "All that matters is that we're together."

"You mean that?" He looked down at her, his features relaxing into a grin at her nod.

"I love you, Solen, and that isn't up for debate, but we'll be having a talk about communication after this is over." She gave him a pointed look that went with her tone.

"Promise." He kissed her softly.

A growl caught both their attention, they turned to see Draken face to face with Livinia, who was standing her ground while still holding up a weakened Rikar. "You're the one who kidnapped Cali and my brother."

Rikar straightened up enough to stand between Livinia and Draken. "She helped us escape, brother, she didn't have to but she did. The Ancients won't be looking fondly upon her for doing that." Draken stepped back but shot Livinia a dark look before helping his brother stand straighter and growling.

"How could you let them do this to you?" Draken growled at his brother.

"You know me." Rikar attempted to grin at his

brother but it fell short. "Always the first one to volunteer, even when it isn't in my best interest."

Draken chuckled as he helped his brother stand taller. "Yeah, well next time, don't volunteer."

"Let's not have a next time." Calista smiled at them both. "Let's get out of here and go back to Ara."

"Afraid we can't let that happen."

CHAPTER 17

Standing there between them and the hangar were Risa, Ryno and Riso in front of a group of nasty looking Champions. Calista didn't see Ricci around, so his position as Ryno called it must not be out in the open. "This isn't good."

Draken let out a growl from behind her and she heard Rikar's faint growl as well. "Stay here, brother." Turning she saw Draken place Rikar against the wall behind them.

"No." Rikar growled attempting to push off the wall, his brother's hand stopped him.

"You'll fight when you're capable." He smirked at his brother, who glared at him. "Let me rephrase that, don't volunteer for foolish things that keep you from the fight. Until you're able, sit back and enjoy the show."

"They're in the way of the hangar." Rikar raised a brow at his brother who continued to smirk.

"No one leaves unless we allow it," Risa spoke as the Champions started to move closer to them.

"Consider this our permission slip." Draken started to glow, a hazy vision of his dragon appearing as he slammed his hand on the metal floor. A tremor was sent out before them towards the Ancients and Champions. Pillars, columns, walls and the ground shook as the Ancients and Champions lost their footing. Some managed to keep themselves from completely landing on the floor but most collapsed from Draken's mighty blow.

Calista stared at Draken, an astonished expression on her face. "Draken, you cracked a joke!" She started to laugh. "You haven't done that in so long."

He flashed her one of his half grins with a wink. "I'll have to try to do that more often then."

"You better." She nudged him with her shoulder.

"Hey!" Solen frowned at her but she just laughed. She didn't care, right now she had all the ones she loved with her and they were going to find a way home whether the Ancients liked it or not. "My Spider," he said possessively.

"Yeah, well your mystic tried to get rid of your Spider," Calista told him.

"What?" Solen had pulled a silver and green bow from behind him when she said that, but her words had him pausing.

"We can deal with her when we're out of here and back on Ara," Rikar suggested weakly.

"Best advice I've heard so far." Kaine moved from behind the wall Rikar was leaning against. "Stryx is waiting for the shield to drop so he can get us out of here." He placed his hand on the ground and just as he had in her dream, he sent streaks of energy along the floor towards the Ancients and Champions who were attempting to right themselves. They were now jumping, some screeching in pain that didn't get out of the way in time.

"If the shield goes down, we won't be able to breathe." Calista frowned at him but he only grinned.

"Yeah, because we didn't think about that." Kaine rolled his eyes at her, earning him glares from both brothers and a menacing growl from Draken. "Hey, say something foolish like that and you'll get a sarcastic response." Kaine flashed an unrepentant smile as he pulled a small metal ball from his pocket. Closing his fist around the ball they watched as his hand glowed brightly. Pulling his hand back he threw the ball towards the Ancients and Champions. It exploded above their heads. "I care more about getting us off this rock alive than feelings right now, and I'm not apologizing for it."

"Finally, someone who speaks sense." Livinia looked impressed, Rikar's expression darkened as he frowned at her.

"Let's argue about this when we get back home. Until we get back on our ship, we're sitting ducks." Solen shook his head as he pulled out an arrow from behind him, nocking the arrow and letting it fly at the ground beneath some Champions that were advancing towards them. The floor beneath them froze and all but one slipped, falling down. Unfortunately, the one still standing started to glow red, melting the ice at his feet. "We need to get past these guys and take out the shield or we're not getting off this rock."

"What about getting one of their ships?" Rikar frowned at him.

"Their ships are programmed only to operate if an Ancient is on the ship." Solen let loose another arrow at the hot head coming towards them. It exploded on contact, erupting into a fluffy ball of retardant that engulfed the Champion. "I don't know about you but I would rather just take these guys out than try to kidnap one in the hopes we can get them to operate one of their ships."

"Solen!" Calista shouted as one of the Champions suddenly appeared behind him. She raised a hand intent on sending the Champion flying when a bolt of blue plasma hit him in the chest, doing what she had planned to do.

Turning she saw Allen standing there with a small gun like weapon in his outstretched hand, grinning at his brother. "Seems you should practice what you preach bro, distractions can get you killed."

Solen frowned at him. "What're you doing here? You should be back on the ship with Stryx and the others waiting for the sign."

"I didn't join the corps to sit out just because big brother was worried," Allen told him as he moved forward. Kaine's eyes went wide at Allen's words, he turned away letting a couple more energized balls fly towards two Champions who were running towards him, their limbs extending in length as they reached out to grasp him. The balls exploded on impact, the lengthened limbs shrinking back while the Champions let out shrieks of pain.

"How about doing what your commanding officer ordered you to do? We need a sharpshooter on board that could cover us when we board." Solen's bow turned into a staff as he slammed it into the gut of a big Champion nearby. As the Champion doubled over in pain, he brought the staff up into his face, knocking him back and out for the count.

"Allie can do that," Allen protested.

"Allie will be watching for any debris that could damage the ship." Solen bit out, turning around, aiming his bow to shoot out another arrow that let out a net that covered the stretchy Champions that had recovered from Kaine's powered balls.

"I didn't know," Allen said, looking crestfallen.

"You didn't need to know," his brother bit out in frustration. "You just needed to follow orders."

"Reprimand later. Fight now," Calista told him as she held out her hand, manipulating the Champions that were struggling in the net, so that their molecules turned into the same metal as the floor. Merging them with the floor beneath them. "I would like to get away from this place, soon."

Allen grinned at her. "You got it, sis!" Ignoring his brother's disgruntled look, he joined the fight with his gun that would change size and features. Blue plasma bolts flying, taking out Champions that were attempting to stop them. The amount of Champions they were fighting showed that even with all that Solen had been attempting to free, he wasn't even close to freeing them all.

Champions with different powers were coming at them. Fire shooting, water spraying, wind gusting and so much more were facing Calista, Solen, Livinia, Draken, Kaine, Allen and a weakened Rikar. "What's our goal?"

One of Livinia's braids moved to point towards the tallest metal tower that stood past the hangar, behind the Ancients with their Champions and in the center of the platform. "That is the control tower that controls not only the shield protecting this fortress but is also controlling their ships." She stayed her position next to a frustrated looking Rikar. Her hair whipped around her as she watched all the fighting going on.

"Great, so all we have to do is to get past the legions of Ancients with their Champions to get to the tower in the center of this base." Calista felt as if the floor had just tilted on them. "How are we going to do that?"

"By working together and kicking their asses." Draken growled as he transformed into his mighty dragon, the air all around him crackling with blue energy as his eyes glowed. He leapt over their companions, landing with a crash in front of some Champions who shrank back from his imposing image. His mighty clawed hand swiped two Champions who were attempting to use their powers against him, projectiles bouncing off his scaled armor while they went flying across the platform into unconscious heaps.

Solen was taking out Champions with his arrows and bow that would not only switch to a staff but a spear as well. He never missed. Although the Champions managed to get a lucky hit on him. One Champion that could multiply herself swept Solen's feet from underneath him, landing a powerful blow to his chest as he landed. With Solen temporarily winded the Champion went for the killing blow, Allen sent a plasma bolt that hit the Champion and disintegrated her but an identical one just appeared ready to finish the job. Calista leapt into the air, landing on the Champion's shoulder, pressing her into the floor by manipulating the air around them until she had become a permanent part of the floor.

With a grin., she helped Solen up. "How would I be able to make you grovel for years if you let yourself get killed?" she said.

"Can't have that." He grimaced as he stood, kissing her soundly then grinning at his brother. "Yeah, that might've bailed you out." Allen gave a hand flip salute before turning and aiming his gun that was longer than any gun Calista had seen back home. He let loose a volley of plasma bolts that hit their marks.

They advanced towards the Champions, taking them out, even as the Champions sent their best attacks against them. Livinia stayed by Rikar's side as the others battled through the Champions towards their target. As Calista watched Draken's dragon take out Champion after Champion. One that looked like a metal porcupine advanced upon Draken, the spines melted in the blue fire that Draken spewed, melting the Champion to the deck.

"We're going to do this!" Kaine shouted excitedly as he threw some energized balls into one of the ships that were on the edge of the hangar as they were getting closer to the control tower.

"We're winning!" Allen shouted. "Way to go, Dragon man!" The Ancients looked spooked as Draken started advancing on them. Turning, they rushed away, shouting for their Champions to protect them. But their Champions were barely protecting themselves as each attack they sent Draken's way just ended in their demise.

"Pull out the cannon!" The Ancients started shouting in fear as they ran to get away from Draken.

"We need to get out of here, now!" Rikar's voice was still weak as Livinia was doing her best to help him move forward, ignoring her suggestions that he not exert himself in his weakened state. "That cannon is their ultimate weapon; it'll destroy us."

The weapon the Champions pulled out looked lethal with its long barrel that was pointed right at them.

Kaine smirked. "Any weapon they bring I'll light up." Leaning down he placed his hand on the ground, energy arcing from his fingertips towards the weapon.

"Stop." Rikar attempted to stop him but his voice was still weak.

Calista watched as the energy moved from the ground up through the wheels on the cannon until the cannon was glowing completely. She felt a glimmer of hope, this could work.

"He's dead." Rikar shook his head looking regretful.

She frowned at his words; it looked as if it was working to her. "What do you mean?"

He looked at her. "They drained me until there was nothing left, that is what they're going to be shooting from that cannon." He looked back towards Kaine who was grinning at the now glowing cannon.

"Say goodbye to your little toy." The triumph on Kaine's face as he looked at the Ancients would be infectious if not for Rikar's words.

The glowing receded from the shell of the weapon into the barrel of the cannon where it grew menacingly bright. Calista felt a shiver of dread crawl up her spine as she looked over at Kaine. She slowly shook her head as the mouth of the cannon glowed even brighter. Slowly she mouthed the word no as Solen looked from her to Kaine. Solen moved towards his friend but it was too late as the sound of the cannon firing echoed all around them. Kaine's eyes widened as he realized what was happening.

It all happened in slow motion, no one could stop the events as they played out in front of them. The warnings from the Ancients about their weapon echoed in Calista's head as she watched, her whole body tensing in terror at what was happening. The bright light shot straight for Kaine, Calista's hand went to her mouth as her breathing stopped, she could hear the shouts but they seemed so far away. She thought of Brooke back on Ara, expecting her brother to return. Kaine's family who had welcomed them with open arms, whose son wouldn't be returning because of them. This couldn't be happening.

A roar could be heard before the beam reached Kaine, and as they all watched, at the last second, Draken shoved him out of the way, Kaine falling to the side, alive. Draken wasn't as lucky, the beam hit him square in the chest, knocking him to the ground. As Calista watched the mighty dragon shift back into the man.

CHAPTER 18

NO!" Rikar roared. It took all his energy but he scrambled towards his brother with Livinia's help. He knelt there next to his brother, whose complexion was waning with each second. Calista stumbled forward as her vision blurred with tears, her head shaking as the reality of what happened started to sink in. "Draken." Rikar looked down at his brother, his chest heaving with emotion.

"Hey there, little brother." Draken looked up at him with a weak smile. "Couldn't let you be the first to volunteer again."

"You're going to be all right," Rikar told him, his hands moving to the blackened hole in his brother's chest as Calista slowly moved her feet towards Draken, moving almost robotic.

"You and I both know that's not going to happen," Draken spoke, his voice growing weaker and breathing going shallow.

"Yes, it is." Rikar's voice shook as he placed his hands on Draken's chest, a very dull glow emanating from them.

Draken grabbed his brother's hand, giving a shake of his head as Calista fell to her knees on the opposite side staring down at him. "It's too late, you know that, even if you don't want to admit it. Let me talk." Draken told him when Rikar opened his mouth. "I love you brother, you've always been the one to keep me grounded when I fly off the handle. You've been there for me through it all, I never said thank you."

"You never had to," Rikar told him, swallowing hard.

"I should have." Draken breathed out. "Thank you, brother. Thank you for being there for me during the darkest times when I didn't know whether I would walk in the sun again." Rikar nodded, not saying anything as he couldn't trust his voice. "Take care of Kimi and Calton, they deserved so much better." Calista frowned at that comment but said nothing as Rikar nodded again. Then Draken looked at her, it felt as if time had reversed itself, he was smiling at her just as he had during her first time in Atlantis. That look of playfulness in his small smile, how she had missed that. "Hey princess," he greeted her, his hand reaching for her cheek. She took his hand and held it to her cheek, the tears falling, no longer did she try to stop them. "I'm glad you're here."

"Hey there, little man." Calista frowned when Draken looked over her shoulder with a grin. "I should've known you wouldn't listen." She moved her head to see Eon stepping forward, from where she didn't know. He knelt down next to Calista at Draken's head staring silently down at the man he always looked up to. "You take care of your sister for me," Draken told him and he nodded. "Make sure that one treats her right." Draken gave a weak nod towards Solen.

Eon nodded and spoke in a raspy voice. "I will."

Draken nodded then looked back at Calista, his hand starting to grow heavy in Calista's grasp as his breathing slowed even more. "I love you, Calista. I always have. I'm sorry if I ever made you doubt it. I was only trying to protect you."

"I love you too, Draken. I don't want to lose you," Calista told him through tears, sniffling as they coursed down her cheeks.

"Unfortunately, we don't always get what we want," he said, his pallor going even paler as his breathing slowed more. Solen reached them, placing a comforting hand on Calista's shoulder as he stared down at his friend. Draken looked at him. "You take care of her, brother, or I will come back from the underworld to kick your ass."

Solen nodded. "I will, brother."

Kaine appeared standing behind Rikar, Draken saw him and with his last breath he told him, "You're welcome." With those words, his eyes closed, letting out his last breath, his body went still. Calista hung her head as tears fell, not caring that they were sitting there on the ground in the middle of a battlefield. She clung to

Draken's lifeless hand, holding it to her cheek as she cried, not knowing what was going on around her.

A bright light had her looking up to see Rikar encased in a golden sphere of sorts, rings with numerical numbers swirling around Rikar that resembled some of the time pieces she had seen in her grandfather's sanctum. She looked over at Eon to see him staring at Rikar, his hand outstretched towards him. Looking back at Rikar she saw that the bruises from earlier were fading away, his weakened expression was becoming stronger as he straightened up. When the glow receded and the rings faded there was a completely healed Rikar.

Calista looked back at Eon to find him looking at her, his eyes full of sorrow. She wanted to reach out to hold him to her, comfort him as she had done many times before. As she was about to, a most astonishing thing occurred. She was still staring into his eyes but his features started to age until she was no longer looking into the eyes of a boy, but that of a young man.

This young man looked to Rikar and spoke in a mature voice that matched his new persona, "you take care of them, I'll get everyone to the ship."

Rikar stood and nodded to him, looking one last time at his brother before turning and walking towards the Ancients who were now yelling at their Champions to ready the cannon for another attack. Calista frowned at Eon. "What's going on, Eon?"

Instead of answering her, Eon stood up and closed

his eyes. Within minutes they were all encased within another golden ball with similar rings surrounding them. Calista looked around to see that Livinia, Kaine, Allen, Solen and Draken were with her and Eon in the ball. She looked for Rikar and saw him transform into his dragon, but this dragon was much more than she had ever seen before. His light blue had darkened so that he looked more black than blue. His wings spread out with talons on the end of each point, the wings themselves could rival those on the airplanes that traveled the skies back home while the talons looked pointed and deadly. The scales that adorned his body were dark and they moved in unison around his body, as if to make sure he was well protected.

She didn't know what her brother had done, if, in fact, it was even her brother's doing. But whatever had happened, this wasn't Rikar's normal dragon. Each step he took sent shockwaves across the ground. Shockwaves they couldn't feel within Eon's bubble. One of the Champions ran towards him, growing in size the closer he got to Rikar, until he was almost as large as Rikar's dragon. When he leapt towards Rikar, one of Rikar's clawed hands reached out and grabbed the Champion by his throat. He barely gave the Champion a glance as he squeezed and snapped his neck, letting him fall lifeless to the ground as he continued to move forward towards the Ancients and their Cannon.

Calista felt a cold trickle down her spine watching

Rikar, she had never seen him so ruthless, not even in the battle with the first Ancients that came to Atlantis. She worried if this had changed him, even as she understood why it would. It had always been Rikar and Draken or Draken and Rikar. You never got one without the other, now there was only Rikar.

Rikar stopped by the control tower that they had been heading towards, the one they wanted to take down so their ship could come and rescue them. He reached out and grasped the tower in his grip. With one mighty yank, he pulled it from the floor, the wires sparking as they ripped apart. The shield started to crackle before it disappeared and Eon floated the bubble from the fortress into space. "No!" Calista yelled at Eon. "We can't leave Rikar!" Livinia looked at her then to Eon before running towards him with her hair moving only to end up contained in a bubble within this bubble. "Eon!" Calista shouted, but her brother paid her no attention as the bubble moved further from the floating fortress where they could barely see Rikar.

As those in the bubble watched, Rikar opened his mouth and out came a bright blue light that surrounded all of the fortress and then exploded right before their eyes. "NO!" Calista started shaking her head, not believing what they were seeing. Not Rikar too. Was his pain too much?

"Spider!" Solen's voice sounded as if it was far away as he attempted to talk to her, the roaring in her ears deafened all sound around her. She couldn't believe what she was seeing. She had lost them both. She looked up at Solen, saw the concern in his eyes and then nothing.

As everything around her slowly started to turn dark, she heard Solen continue to call to her, "Spider?"

Calista opened her eyes seeing Solen looking down at her, seated on the edge of the bed she was laying in. She rose then looked around her, praying it was all a dream. "Rikar?" She looked at Solen.

"He's in the med bay, but he's alive." Solen's voice held sorrow.

"Draken?" She asked, fearful of the answer that she saw shining in his eyes.

Solen shook his head. "He didn't make it, Rikar and Eon are with him now."

She moved from the bed, brushing off Solen's attempt at restraining her. "I should be there with them."

He gave a hesitant nod. "Fine, but I'm going as well."

Looking into his eyes, holding back her tears she nodded in agreement. "You were friends, you should be there."

"He was my brother," Solen replied.

Eon was leaning against the counter in the med bay as they entered. Rikar was standing next to his brother, staring down at him, saying nothing. Livinia was off to the side, watching. Calista moved to stand with Rikar, placing a comforting hand on his shoulder although she knew not what to say. Either Rikar wasn't acknowledging her presence or he didn't even realize she was there. Whichever it was, she couldn't blame him. She lay her head against his shoulder for a few moments in an act of comfort before leaving him with his brother while she moved to embrace hers. Solen stood on the other side of the bed, staring down at his friend silently.

That was how Kaine found them when he entered, he gave a nod of respect towards Draken then looked at Solen and gestured he needed a word with him. Solen breathed in and touched Draken's shoulder before moving out of the med room to speak with Kaine. Calista and Eon followed, leaving Rikar and Livinia in the room.

"I haven't said anything to anyone on Ara about Lizbet during our transmissions." Kaine was saying as they entered the galley. "All they know is that we have a casualty and we should be home within a day or so."

Solen nodded. "I think that would be best, right now emotions are going to be riding high enough without adding that to it." Kaine grasped Solen's arm in a comforting grip and turned to leave them.

"I guess I should introduce you two." Calista looked between Eon and Solen. "Solen, this is my little brother Eon. Eon, this is Solen." Solen held out a hand in greeting that Eon ignored, although he did nod in greeting. Calista sighed. "Eon, be nice."

Eon opened his mouth to speak but a crash outside the room had them rushing out to see what was the matter. Calista's heart stopped as she saw Rikar standing there with his forearm pressing against Kaine's throat, rage burning in his eyes. After seeing what he did to the Ancients back on their meteor, she worried what he would do to Kaine. "Rikar!" She shouted moving forward but Solen held her back, placing himself between her and them.

"It's your fault that my brother is dead!" Rikar growled into Kaine's face.

Kaine stared at him with sorrow in his eyes. "I know and nothing I can say will bring him back or make this situation better."

"This isn't his fault, Rikar." Solen attempted to ease the situation.

"Yes, it is," Kaine spoke, his voice full of regret.

"Kaine," Solen protested.

"You know it is, Solen." Kaine's gaze never wavered from Rikar's as he spoke. "It's my fault and that's something I'll have to live with for the rest of my life. If I hadn't attempted something foolhardy, Draken would still be here."

"We don't know that." Solen attempted to diffuse the situation one more time.

"Rikar, he's not the one you're mad at," Calista told him softly.

Rikar stood straight, releasing Kaine who gulped in air, rubbing his throat. Looking over at Calista, Rikar's words were hard. "You're right." With that he turned, walking back into the med unit, with Livinia following him after a brief hesitation.

Chapter 19

The ship was quiet, they had escaped the Ancients and were heading back to Ara. But the price that they had paid was too high. Rikar hadn't left his brother's side after that confrontation with Kaine. He didn't even acknowledge anyone that entered the med room. Livinia had become his constant silent companion.

Eon spent his time between the med room and the cargo hold where he had been staying since becoming a stowaway. He never truly explained how he managed to get on the ship, just said he had been there watching from his little hideout. She had a feeling that he had a hand in the incidents that happened which they had no explanations for at the time, not that any of that mattered right now.

Calista leaned her forehead against the cool glass of the windows in the galley where she was hiding out from everyone. Solen had been giving her space, and he and Kaine spent most of their time on the bridge with the others. Not many wanted to be around them, either giving them their space or just not knowing what to say. A noise by the door had Calista moving her head to see Livinia standing there watching her.

"Well, at least now I know why you came back for us." Calista tilted her head looking at Livinia.

"Do you really?"

Calista couldn't even find it in herself to chuckle, she just nodded. "You have feelings for Rikar, whether they're love or not." Calista shrugged.

"So, you think you have me figured out huh?" Livinia questioned her as she moved into the room.

"Tell me I'm wrong." Calista leaned her head back against the padded seat with a sigh, staring out of the window of the ship, not even caring if Livinia answered her or not.

"You are wrong."

Calista didn't turn her head to look at Livinia, she felt as empty as the space she was staring at through the window. "You haven't left his side since we got on this ship," she pointed out.

"And you are not there by his side where you should be," Livinia countered.

Now that got Calista's attention, barely. She turned her head to the side to look at Livinia who was now leaning against the table across from her. "He doesn't seem to want anyone." Was Calista's response. Rikar had barely acknowledged anyone, she wanted to be there for him but she didn't know what to do. He seemed to be mad at everyone, she kind of understood it but dammit, he wasn't the only one hurting.

"Why? Because he does not speak? He is in mourning." Calista opened her mouth to repeat her thoughts but Livinia held up a hand to silence her. Calista closed her mouth but her eyes narrowed as she waited for Livinia to continue. "He is in so much pain right now that he is scared of what he will say if he would dare to speak. Rikar loves you too much and wishes to not cause you any more pain." Calista's expression fell at her words. Livinia stared at her. "He needs you, probably more than you need him."

Swinging her feet around and placing them on the floor she gave Livinia a calculating look. "For someone who cares nothing for the feelings of others, you seem to know a lot about Rikar's."

Livinia stared at her. "Maybe I am starting to like him, but whichever it is, you know I am right."

Calista sighed and nodded. "So, why did you come back and save us? The Ancients won't forget you did that."

"They altered the contract, that is not allowed."

"Is that what your people said as well?" This time Livinia was the one to look away, which was odd. Calista may not have known her long but she did know Livinia wasn't one to look away. "Or did you not even talk to them?"

"My people would agree the Ancients voided the contract due to their last-minute alteration without going through the proper channels." Livinia's words were being spoken very carefully as if she was making sure to choose her words wisely.

"So, that means you haven't broken any of your people's laws then."

"Actually, I have broken several with my latest actions."

"The Ancients broke them first," Calista protested and Livinia just gave a self-deprecating chuckle.

"That will make no difference to my people. I should have gone through the proper channels is what they will say." Livinia looked back at her with a ghost of a smile. "I have never been one for politics, bipartisan takes too long."

"So, you've always been a rebel?" Calista asked; a small smile answered Livinia's ghostly one.

"Usually it works in my favor, but I fear that this time, it will not be excused."

"Why?"

"Because my actions may have endangered one of my own." This time Livinia showed regret in her expression.

"Huh? How?"

"The Ancients' ultimate weapon."

"Rikar destroyed it along with the Ancients, their Champions and their base."

Livinia shook her head, a trickle of dread traveled down Calista's spine. "That was not their only weapon, it was only a prototype. A smaller version of the main one."

"They have a bigger weapon than that one?" Calista swallowed hard at her nod. "Great."

"One of my people was transporting the energy they siphoned from Rikar, they only kept a small amount for the test. He is taking it to the Ancient's lead ship where they are waiting for him, along with instructions on how to bypass Ara's defenses."

"Lizbet told them how to bypass Ara's defenses?" Calista knew she was jealous of her but did she seriously sign the death sentence for all of her family and friends.

Livinia shook her head. "No, it was I that had done that."

"Oh."

Livinia nodded. "And now, due to my transgression, my fellow assassin could be walking into a death sentence of his own."

"Oh." Calista now understood the quandary that surely must be going on inside of Livinia. "I'm sorry for your friend but if you hadn't come back when you did, I don't know that any of us would've made it off that ship."

"I do not regret my decision; I never regret any decision I make," Livinia told her. Calista didn't say anything about the look of regret she was sure she had seen earlier.

Not sure what to say, Calista decided to change the subject. "So, do you think the longer you stay away from your home world, that you'll start getting more feelings?"

"More?" Livinia raised a brow.

"I said what I said," Calista told her.

"I do not know; this is the longest I have been away. I guess we will have to see." Livinia looked out the window. "When a child is born on my world, there is no coddling. From the moment the child opens its eyes, it is being observed and tested to determine its place in our society."

"Its place?" It sounded so cold.

Livinia nodded. "Assassin, warrior, caretaker, judge, executor, politician and so forth."

"Politician?" Thinking of the politicians back home, Calista couldn't see how they could function in such a by the book society that has no feelings. Earth's politicians couldn't function without their drama, whether it's self-created or just readily available.

Livinia inclined her head. "Yes, they decide the roles of my people as well as the rules. There is not a decision that happens in my world without a politician's knowledge. To do so, is to court disaster upon you and your family."

"I stand corrected, that sounds exactly like our politicians." Calista couldn't stop herself from speaking out loud. Livinia frowned at her but she just shook her head. "Talking to myself." She laughed at Livinia's confused expression. "So, your roles in society isn't handed down through genetics?"

Livinia shook her head. "No, it is clearly on merit. By the time a child hits adolescence, their role in our society is already determined. They have no doubts."

"Can anyone else on your world fight with their hair like you?" Calista couldn't stop herself from asking, she had been curious ever since she saw what her hair could do.

Livinia scrunched up her nose in thought, something Calista was sure hadn't happened before. "Not sure honestly, I know we are granted certain gifts based on our roles we are given. Some get more than one."

"Like you?" At the questioning look she continued. "Your hair for one, and let's not forget you being able to disappear or become invisible like you do. And any other skill you may possess."

"As an assassin, I have the skills needed for me to do my job," Livinia said ignoring the slight prompting from Calista about any other skills.

"You've never wanted to be anything else?" Calista asked her.

"What do you mean?"

"Ever wanted to be a caretaker?"

"Why? I was trained as an assassin, that is my role."

"So, you never get the chance to choose your own path or even change it if you chose?" At Livinia's shake of her head Calista sighed. "How sad."

"Why sad? We could choose wrong and then be of no help to our society. This is much more scientific and takes away any confusion."

Calista thought about trying to explain the benefits of the freedom to choose one's own destiny but she wasn't sure Livinia would understand. Maybe she would once she was able to experience it. She was sure Rikar would be bringing her home with them. At that thought she felt her chest start to tighten. She looked at the door.

As if Livinia could read her mind she nodded. "You should go to him, he needs you just as much as you need him right now."

Calista nodded, rose and turned to leave, only pausing to say, "thank you." With that she walked out of the galley and down the hall to the med bay where she found Rikar in the same spot. Standing next to Draken, staring down at him. She moved closer to him and put her arm around his waist, sending a silent prayer he didn't rebuff her. When he slid an arm around her, she laid her head on his shoulder and stood there with him. Silent tears falling as they stayed there in silence.

She felt more than heard Eon enter the med bay. He walked over to stand with them silently. Not sure how much later it was that Solen entered but he stayed silent as well, standing there. Eon was the first one to speak, it was still odd for her to hear his more mature voice after thinking her little brother would never grow up. Then again, the death of someone you held dear was a life altering experience.

"I was there when he met Kimi."

This got their attention, even Rikar's.

"She's a daughter of Ares, you know." Rikar nodded but Calista felt a punch in the gut at hearing that.

"I didn't know." Calista hadn't thought about any of the Greek Gods or Goddesses after she left there.

"Yup, he wanted nothing to do with her no matter how much she attempted to get his attention." Eon's lips twitched. "So, she made his scales pink for one full year, until he finally broke down and talked to her."

"That's why he refused to shift into a dragon that one year?" Rikar looked at Eon with an incredulous look. "He never told me that. I could've had real fun with that knowledge." Calista liked seeing the smile on Rikar's face, even if it didn't last very long.

"Pink?" She looked over at her brother who was nodding.

"Her mother is Aphrodite." He gave a small shrug. "Not that she advertises that fact, she didn't inherit her mom's girliness."

"Or airheadness." Rikar imposed.

Calista looked up at him. "Is that even a word?"

Rikar shrugged. "It fits."

Calista nodded.

"Remember that time he set up colored octopus ink bombs in Cael's temple in retaliation for the eggs in his bed?" Solen said with a faraway looking grin.

Rikar gave a small chuckle. "He didn't expect Malis to come looking for Cael."

"Yeah, he was hiding from her for weeks after." Solen grinned. "Malis was more colorful than any of the coral beds."

"Is that why mom always makes dad enter his temple first?" Calista asked, Eon looking just as curious. Both Solen and Rikar laughed at her question.

"Yeah," Rikar told her. "I really thought she was going to make a dragon rug out of Draken that time." Calista laughed, but before she could talk about any memory she had of Draken, Kaine's voice interrupted them via the intercom.

"Ara in sight, everyone get ready for landing."

CHAPTER 20

The beauty of Ara that had drawn Calista in before now seemed hollow to her. When they landed, Draken's body was taken to a hut where he was placed on a ceremonial slab with reverence. He was covered with a silk blue cover that had golden images of dragons flying etched within the fabric. Grint offered a warrior funeral for Draken to Rikar. Rikar told him that he was sure that Draken would be honored.

So now the whole village was preparing for Draken's funeral that would take place as soon as the light faded. Calista and Livinia had told them about how the weapon that Rikar had destroyed was only a prototype and that the main one was probably being readied as they stood there. Livinia did say that according to all her sources they should have a good few days before the attack happened but that it was coming. She also admitted to her role in not only the kidnapping but being the reason that the Ancients were now able to penetrate their defenses. Grint told her that it mattered not, she had been crucial in the rescue and was with them fighting now. That was what mattered.

Considering that only hours before he had been told of the treachery from his own daughter, Calista thought it was very big of him to not condemn Livinia.

"I should be at the funeral with my father." Lizbet's angry voice could be heard from behind Calista. She turned to see Lizbet standing outside of the ceremonial hut where Draken's body lay. "I'm the Mystic of Ara, I'm needed."

"No, what you are is a traitor." Rikar growled at her. What was that girl doing? "You may have not pulled the trigger on the weapon that killed my brother but your hand still has his blood dripping from it. You should be thanking Ara that you still breathe." When Rikar turned and walked away, Calista realized she had been holding her breath. She truly worried that Rikar would've done more than growled at Lizbet, not that he didn't have the right but it would've made things very awkward.

Lizbet stared in shock at Rikar's retreating figure. She turned to her father. "Father, please."

"You'll not attend tonight's funeral, you will not disrespect his brother's passing. I pray you find forgiveness within yourself for the atrocity that you have committed against our people. I can't make this go away for you, I'm afraid." The inner struggle that Grint was feeling was evident in his expression. The pain of not being able to take away his daughter's grievance. "I love you, my Lizbet. I will always love you, but this is something you are going to have to atone for. You'll need to beg for

Ara's forgiveness for the betrayal of your people, for the consequences of your actions. Until you do that, I won't be able to help you, but know that I'll always love you."

"Father?" Lizbet stared in disbelief as he turned away from her and moved with the other clerics of Ara as they moved to ready the village for the funeral. She turned and saw Calista standing there, she glared at her. "You!" Her face burned with anger.

"Lizbet, this isn't her fault." Solen moved forward.

Lizbet turned on him with a feral snarl. "Heaven forbid anyone say anything bad about your precious *Spider.*" Her lips sneered over his pet name for Calista. "I can be ridiculed, slandered and threatened but not one menacing whisper in her direction." Her voice shook with her emotion.

"You betrayed us all by your actions," he told her.

"I betrayed you?" She stared at him with wide eyes shining with anger. "You betrayed me!" She practically screamed at him. "You promised me that you would come back for me! Instead, you replaced me with her!" She pointed at Calista, her eyes wild in her anger and hurt.

"I tried to save you the embarrassment of a failed joining ceremony and the repercussions that would follow." Solen told her, attempting to get her to calm down but it seemed once the floodgates had been opened, there was no closing them.

"You mean that you were trying to save yourself. I would've given up my power for you." Lizbet's voice was carrying so that everyone in town could plainly hear this discussion. Some had even given up the act of trying to look as if they weren't listening.

"I would never ask that of you."

"You didn't have to."

"I no longer had the same feelings for you." Solen looked pained as he attempted to reason with her. "I never meant to hurt you, Lizbet."

"Too late."

"And that makes it okay for you to betray our people?"

"I didn't mean to betray our people; I wanted her gone." Lizbet pointed to Calista who was starting to feel as if she was an interloper. "Then you would come to care for me again."

"That's not how it works." Solen told her and turned away as several of her father's clerics came to remove her from the situation.

"I did it for us!" She screamed and ran down the path from the town before the clerics could remove her.

Calista watched Solen walk into the forest and after a brief moment or two she followed him. He was leaning against a tree looking lost and bereft. She moved to him and placed a hand on his shoulder. He turned to look at her. "I never realized."

"You didn't want to," she informed him.

He sighed, laying his head against hers. "You're right."

"I know." She held onto him as they stood there beneath the leaves of the tree where she could feel the Aggies watching them. She had dealt with loss before, she couldn't be as old as she was and not. But never had she dealt with a loss this close before. Tonight she would be saying goodbye to a man who was like a brother to her, a man who should be standing with them in the battle that was to come. She sighed, closing her eyes as Solen held her to him.

The light had faded and now the village was bathed in a beautiful glow from Ara's fire that was glowing brighter than she had ever seen it. Calista could feel the heat of the flames as she stood with Rikar, Solen, Livinia and Eon outside the hut where Draken's body lay. They were all dressed in silken finery that complimented the silk blanket over Draken's body. The whole village was out in their best to honor the great warrior, Draken. The clerics were moving the body from the hut but were stopped by the Aggies who suddenly appeared.

Calista looked up at Solen but he seemed surprised by their appearance as well. Sanders moved to stand in front of Rikar where he bowed. "Us Aggies would like the honor of transporting the great warrior and hero of Ara to his final resting place with Ara." Calista blinked back tears as Rikar nodded his approval.

Bastion, Juna and the other Aggies moved to take the

place of the clerics while Sanders led them forward towards the fire. Gentle music played as they walked to the fire with Rikar, Livinia, Eon, Solen and Calista following. The Aggies moved with ease as if they were not small and Draken wasn't the big man he was, until the wooden gurney was in the fire that started to glow brighter.

"Rest thy warrior within Ara's embrace.

Within Ara you will find your place.

Your battles have been fought; your wars are done.

Rest within Ara as one of her sons."

Not only was Velva singing but the Aggies joined as well, creating a harmony as the fire grew brighter and bigger until it formed a mighty dragon. Calista looked up through watery eyes, seeing Draken's dragon looking down at them in the flames.

"Sing the song of Ara,

Within her arms we thrive.

Sing the song of Ara,

Our warrior's last paradise."

The fiery dragon flew into the air then swooped down and flew around the village, weaving through the throng of people that were watching reverently. When it passed by Calista she felt a warm sensation on her cheek as if Draken was kissing her goodbye one last time. Then she watched as the fiery dragon seemed to merge with Rikar. Then before their eyes they saw Rikar transform into his blue watery dragon and almost dance with the fiery one of Draken's one last time.

"Sing the song of Ara,
Within her arms we thrive.
Sing the song of Ara,
Our warrior's last paradise."

With those words the fiery dragon launched into the air and dived into the fire of Ara, where they could no longer see Draken's body. Grint stood up in front of the fire, moving his hands in a ceremonial manner before announcing to all, "Our warrior is with Ara."

It was quiet all around, everyone was in their homes resting before tomorrow. Tomorrow they would all be preparing for the upcoming war that was heading to Ara. Tonight, they were supposed to be sleeping. Except every time Calista closed her eyes, she saw Draken's lifeless body. So, now here she was, sitting in a chair by the window with her knees drawn to her chest and her arms wrapped around them. A movement by the door had her turning her head to see Rikar standing in her doorway. "Rikar, I don't feel like talking." She told him, her exhaustion evident in her voice.

"That's fine." He said moving into the room without waiting for an invite and taking a seat on her bed. "Don't talk, just listen."

"I don't feel like doing that either." She turned her head away from him to look back out the window, hoping he would take the hint.

"Well, as a great dragon once said, unfortunately, we don't always get what we want."

His words felt like a blow to the gut. With a glare she looked at him. "And you're supposed to be the easy-going brother."

"Stuff the smart-ass remarks and listen."

She sighed. "Fine." Anything to get him to leave, she knew he was hurting and she really hated being like this but she was tired. The past few days have been an emotional roller coaster ride, and the next few days weren't going to be any better so she just wanted to be left alone for a bit.

"Draken loved you," he told her. She had to suppress the urge to tell him to shut up and leave. This wasn't a talk she was ready to have.

"Yeah, he told me that right before he died." She gave him a hard stare, not understanding why he was bringing this up. It wasn't going to change anything.

"You really need to listen." He told her with a shake of his head, but she just looked away from him. "Draken, he loved you, almost from the beginning." He continued.

"Maybe at one time he did, in his own way."

"He never stopped loving you."

She wanted to roll her eyes at his words but contained the urge, barely. "Then he had a funny way of showing it. For the past several hundred years he has kept me at arm's length, treating me worse than his past conquests that he always avoided as if I had wronged him in some way. Any attempt of attention I tried to give him was met with rejection." She looked at him. "He treated me like an unwanted harpy."

"You were never that to him."

"Could've fooled me." She closed her eyes and leaned her head back, wanting this conversation to be done with.

"Looks like he did."

She barely bit back her frustrated groan. "Rikar, you're sounding worse than a damn prophet. If you have something to say just spit it out."

Rikar sighed. "How much do you remember after Solen left?"

She shrugged. "I was learning who I was and coming to terms with being a goddess of Atlantis."

"Really?"

She ignored the cynicism in that question. "Until you and Draken," she paused in her words as she spoke. "Well, mostly Draken kept badgering me to leave Atlantis." Her lips curled. "That probably should've been the first warning that Draken's attitude towards me had changed."

"You weren't coming to terms with anything." Rikar informed her, holding up a hand when she frowned at him and started to protest. "You went through the motions of living but then you would look up into the sky and become a damn empty shell of yourself. Always looking and waiting for a man who seemed to have forgotten you."

"Is that why Draken seemed to hate Solen?"

"Part of it."

"Part?" Her confusion was written all over her face as she did her best to keep up with what Rikar was trying to say to her.

"Calista," Rikar said, capturing her complete attention when he actually called her by name instead of princess. "When I say Draken loved you, when he told you that before he died, neither of us were speaking of the love a brother has for his sister."

If not for Rikar's quickness she would've ended up on the floor, his words had shaken her to the core as the world around her tilted. He gave a mirthless grin. "I see it finally sank in."

"He never said anything to me, never even hinted. Then why did it feel as if he had grown to hate me?" This time she looked in Rikar's eyes, no longer antagonistic.

"We both wanted you to go out amongst the mortals to give you something else to live for other than waiting for Solen. We hoped that it might bring back the girl who would laugh, play and stand up to us with all her sass. Draken had planned to tell you of his feelings, he was just waiting for you to be whole again." Rikar looked down at his hand that was held in a loose fist as if contemplating something, with a sigh he looked up at her.

Calista said nothing, she wasn't sure what to say so she just waited for him to continue.

"Then came the summons from dear old dad."

She nodded, she did remember that.

"Poseidon wanted you and Draken to be together. He believed that a child born to you both would be very powerful and he had plans for that child." He nodded when Calista's eyes widened. "Yeah, Draken had almost the same expression when father told him what he wanted."

"I'm still not getting how this would make Draken hate me."

"One, we both know how Draken hated being told what to do." Calista nodded although that didn't help her frown. "Two, you know both our feelings when it comes to Poseidon." Another nod, her expression had still not relaxed. "And finally, pops told Draken that he would make sure it happened. Draken wanted to be with you but not if the feelings you had towards him were manufactured by Aphrodite or some type of spell."

"And that is a reason for his attitude towards me?" she asked.

"I tried telling him that he was going about it the wrong way but he felt it was better to push you away, so that way he didn't have to wonder if any affection you showed was actually real." Rikar shrugged.

"Neither of you thought to tell me?" Calista was feeling a slow burn building within her.

Rikar grinned. "So, you could go confront Poseidon?"

"Yes!"

"We didn't want you hurt." Rikar tried to reason with her as he could sense her temper rising.

"You didn't think Draken's attitude towards me would hurt?" She couldn't stop her voice from rising in her anger. "I hurt each time he pushed me away and I didn't know why. I kept thinking it was something I did to him, that I had wronged him somehow."

"It was never you, princess." Rikar stood up and moved towards her but she leapt from the chair and glared at him.

"Would've been nice to know that back then," she told him, her voice hard.

"We were trying to protect you." Rikar appealed to her.

"Next time you want to protect me...don't! I couldn't bear to see you die as well," she told him swirling around and storming from the room, no longer feeling lethargic as her anger rode high.

CHAPTER 21

The fields just outside the village were full of activity as the people of Ara gathered with the Champions who were fighting with them against the Ancients. They knew a battalion of Ancients with their own Champions were on their way, they knew there was a chance they could be outnumbered but no one was going to run. No one.

"Brooke, you're not fighting!"

Calista turned to see Kaine glaring down at Brooke who was there with a bow that she was holding like a pro, staring back up at her brother with determination written all over her face. "Yes, I am!" She declared.

"No!" Kaine's voice thundered all around them.

"Kaine." His mother and father appeared, both with their own weapons as well. His father carried a gun that resembled the one Allen used back on the Ancient's meteor fortress, while his mother carried a staff. "No, no, and no!" He glared at his parents. "She's too young."

"The Ancients aren't going to care about her age, son." His father told him.

"So, you're just going to let her out into the battle where she can die easier?"

"She won't be out in the battle but she will be with your mom and the others who will be guarding the village in case the Ancients or their Champions get through. No child of mine will be cowering in a room, waiting to die." Calista swallowed hard at the firmness in Kaine's father's voice. Even Kaine knew to just nod, although he couldn't stop himself from muttering one last time.

"As long as she stays away from the battlefield."

She looked down at the armor that Solen's mother had helped her get into this morning, she worried about wearing it before the battle and dealing with the heavy clunkiness of armor. Although she was mildly surprised how light and comfortable it was, even more so than Atlantean armor. Which was impressive. The armor moved flawlessly with each movement as if it was part of the person and not attire.

Rikar and Livinia were sparring with each other while Eon watched them. Her and Rikar hadn't spoken at all since their talk about Draken. She wasn't sure there was anything else to say, with this battle coming she didn't have time to try to process the meaning of what Rikar told her. So much has happened in such a short time that she felt overwhelmed. Her hand going to the pendant around her neck, holding it tightly in her hand. Scratch. How she missed him, she wished he were here with her. She needed him.

Looking around, she saw swords that were blazing with flames, cool with an icy film or just lethal. Staffs that transformed from stiff wooden to pliable leather or even sticky tentacles. Bows like Solen's pliable, elegant looking one or crossbows made of metal, wood and crystals would shoot out arrows of different purposes. As she watched the archers with their bows, she noticed something. Each one had a patch with crossing bows somewhere on their armor.

"Hey, Spider." She turned to see Solen there. She frowned when she saw the same patch on his armor, right in the center just under his throat.

"What's that?" she asked, pointing to the patch.

"It's the hunter's symbol?" She raised a brow, looking back at the others with their patches as well.

"I thought you were the only hunter?" she asked him.

He laughed. "No, just the best."

She leaned into him as she looked around seeing Vester and Vernon sparring with each other. Staffs that would change to whatever was needed. While Vester was big and bulky, Vernon was small and wiry. Which made for some interesting practicing moves. Vester seemed to end up on his back more than Vernon did, but Vester still got some good shots in.

"What do you think our chances are?" Calista looked up at Solen, asking the questions that had been burning within her.

Solen looked down at her, his jaw tightened. "We beat them before; we'll beat them again."

"Even with their ultimate weapon?" she countered.

Before he could answer a commotion had them rushing to the edge of the field where they saw legions of armies coming their way. They resembled the other nations that Brooke told her about. Warriors from the Pyre nation with their cracked blackened skin, dark armor and fiery weapons. The Floe nation was walking beside the Pyre nation with their blue dry skin with frosty armor and cold weapons. The Pura nation as well with their aquatic looking armor and glowing weapons. And marching in front of them were the Jinsons, Karkens and Carpes. Small but they were suited up for battle as well.

The Aggies rushed to greet their cousins, all different in so many ways but they embraced one another in greeting. The fields were full of various fighters from many different backgrounds. You have the true children of Ara who happen to be the Aggies, Jinsons, Karkens and Carpes who are miniature in appearance but mighty in spirit. Then you have all the factions of Ara with their differences whether they be in appearances or mannerisms. And you can't forget the Champions that Solen saved from the Ancients who were joining them in their fight.

"Ara called her people to take up arms." Grint appeared, startling Calista who was awed by everything she saw. Her eyes widened when she saw that he was also in armor, a sword sheathed at his waist. She was surprised to see him preparing for battle, which must have shown on her face. His amusement at her expression was evident in his voice. "Even politicians can fight."

"Maybe here," she told him. "But where I come from they would be hiding in a concrete box underneath their home while others died to protect them."

"Then they don't deserve their title." Said Grint.

"You'll get no argument from me." Calista agreed

"Does Gaia not talk to your people?" he asked her. "I knew that many from your world had stopped talking to her, believing in their own superiority. But surely there are some who still listen to her."

"Gaia still has her own apostles." Calista nodded. "Not a legion of them, but she does have some."

"Have you ever spoken with her?" Grint asked.

"No." Calista told him.

"Maybe when you get home, she will talk to you." He suggested.

"Maybe." She smiled at him.

He nodded to her before he moved away to speak with the other factions of Ara.

Solen kissed her temple. "I would love to be there to hear what she has to say to you when you return home triumphant."

Calista laughed. "You will be, now let's go eat before the final hour."

He nodded.

The people of Solen's village opened their homes to the other factions, making changes if needed to help them acclimate and be comfortable. If the villagers were unable to make changes themselves it seemed Ara would lend a hand. Several lava pits appeared around the town for those from the Pyre nations. These pits were bubbling with molten lava but didn't seem to cause any of the other factions any discomfort. In fact, at one of the pits she saw a female from the Floe nation chatting with one of the Pyre nations men as he relaxed in the lava. She was sitting on the outside edge of the pit as if sitting around a pool of cool water.

Watery pools appeared as well, within the water it seemed almost all of the factions could play together. Although certain areas seemed cooler than most while some others were warmer. And you can't forget about the ice palaces that grew from the ground on the outside of the village for those from the Floe nation. Palaces that would rival any of the cartoon royalties on the big screen back on Earth. Calista loved how everyone could come together like this, it was a beautiful sight.

The alarm sounded all through Ara. The Ancients had entered their solar system and were heading to Ara. They had only hours before the Ancients reached them. The lava pits, watery pools, icy palaces and gardens were now empty. Armor donned and weapons at the ready, now everyone was in their strategic positions that were already mapped out. They knew that the Ancients would use their weapon to cut through the magical shield Ara had in place, they knew the damage it could cause.

Rikar stood proud with them on one of the hills outside the village, a hard expression on his face. His lips curled into a snarl as he waited with eagerness for this battle. He had some retribution planned. Livinia was by his side, playing with her knives while her braids moved as if playing in the breeze. Her relaxed manner was very deceiving, Calista knew that Livinia was poised to attack in an instant. Eon stood by her, her little brother all grown up wearing the armor of a warrior. He wore golden bracelets on his wrists, each adorned with a dragon. He told her that he was taking Draken in battle with him.

Kaine and Allen were standing off to the side as they watched the skies. Allen twirling his gun in his hand absently while waiting, currently the size of a handgun from home. Vester and Vernon were positioned a few feet in front of them, Vester standing tall while Vernon knelt down with his elbow resting on his knee. Solen stood on her other side, his hand gripping his bow as he watched the same sky, his hand reaching for hers.

The silence that sat heavy in the air had an eerie feeling as they waited for the invasion, no one spoke, the wind even seemed to understand that a great battle was coming. Solen leaned down until his lips were against her ear. "I love you, Spider. Never forget that."

Those words sent a chill down her spine as she could see Draken's face when he told her he loved her. Not again. Turning she looked into his eyes and shook her head. "You don't get to say that until this battle is over."

Solen nodded with one of his roguish grins. "Will be nice to see Cael again, I've missed him."

"Yeah, well, Dad misses you too." She grinned at him. "So, no pulling anything stupid."

"I'll do my best."

"They're here!" Before she could respond to him the warning announcement rang all around them moments before a flash of bright light tore through the sky and cut through the ground creating a long, deep gouge that extended miles.

CHAPTER 22

The sky filled with ships that landed on the battlefield, Champions rushing from the ships directly into battle with the warriors of Ara. The largest of the ships landed miles from the battlefield, from that ship more Champions departed but they stayed their ground outside the ship and didn't join the battle. Before she could put much more thought into that ship the battle had reached them. Rikar was going between dragon and man as he fought with the Champions foolish enough to challenge him. One female Champion who was shifting from humanoid into a large bird resembling a pterodactyl flew towards him attempting to snag his wing with her claw. Instead, he snatched her by the neck in his mighty grip and slammed her to the ground, creating tremors that had even Livinia frowning at him.

Calista had managed to keep her balance as one of the Champions who had eight arms leapt at her with a shout. She sidestepped him and watched as he slammed the ground creating a small tremor. He glared at her as if it was her fault, she lifted a shoulder with an uncaring gesture that set him off as he jumped up reaching for her. She had been about to show him his folly when Vester appeared and grabbed the guy by one of his many arms, tossing him high into the air. Vernon came running upon them so fast he was nothing but a blur, using Vester as a springboard he launched into the air and came down so fast on the Champion that he accelerated his fall into the ground with a sickening thud. Both the brothers gave her a wink before they started off to find another victim.

"Time to play pretty."

She turned to see a Champion with oily greased back hair and a serpent tongue that he kept sticking out while he hopped from foot to foot.

"Seriously?" She frowned at him, not even wanting to waste her time. She flicked her fingers, sending him flying across the battlefield and away from her. "Go pester someone else."

"You won't be sending me away so easily." She turned, intent on doing just that when she found herself encased in a completely black void. No matter where she stepped there was nothingness there, she couldn't get out of it. She tried to scream but heard nothing, she struck out with her fists but connected with nothing. She felt her anxiety rising as she attempted to break whatever the Champion had done to her.

Don't lose it now, Calista. There has got to be a way out of this. She opened her eyes intent on sending the darkness away when suddenly she was back on the battlefield. Looking over she saw Bastion and Juna jumping on the purple skinned Champion who must have been behind her trip into the darkness. Rainbow colored vines twined around the struggling Champion.

"Let's see how you guys like losing all your senses." The Champion growled, his eyes glowing. Before Calista could react and stop him his body started to film over with an icy film. Two little eyes appeared from the other side of the Champion, peeking out from a furry coat. One of the Jinsons had come to help their cousins. Bastion stood on the Champion, giving Calista a salute.

A flash of lavender had her turning to see Lizbet fighting with a Champion who had a tail that had wrapped around her leg and dragging her down. Her father appeared taking out the Champion's tail with his sword, sending the Champion scurrying away.

All across the field, battles were raging, Champions with all different types of powers doing their best to defeat them. Vernon and Vester were combining their strength and speed together to take down Champion after Champion. Clori was fighting an icy cold Champion with her flames creating clouds of steam. Livinia was battling a Champion who kept stunning her although she got a few good shots in with her braids. Eon rushed up to them, his hands making a twisting motion that ensconced the Champion in a golden bubble. Eon twisted his hands and the Champion reversed in age until she was but a babe.

Allen was fighting with a Champion whose skin was hard as armor while Kaine and Solen had their hands full with Champions who were trying to drown them in water that appeared from the ground and engulfed them. She sent a shockwave along the ground that sent the Champions flying and released Kaine and Solen from a watery grave. They were defeating the Champions; with each battle they were winning but not as flawlessly as they would like. On the ground there were lifeless bodies from both sides.

A scream penetrated the air, it felt as if it had come deep from within Ara herself. When Calista turned around, she gasped out, the Ancients had joined the battle. Riso was standing there holding the lifeless body of Sanderson, his colors completely gone. Behind him she saw the ultimate weapon was being moved onto the battlefield by very strong Champions.

"Bastion!" Juno screamed as the little Aggie went rushing towards the grinning Riso. Calista started to run to him herself but a gust of wind went past her as Vernon reached Bastion first, lifting him up in the air and tossing him back towards Juno. His grin of victory turned into a grimace as he was impaled by a Champion's hand that had turned into a spike.

"No!" Vester shouted as his brother slumped forward down on the ground.

Another Ancient moved forward to touch Vernon before death could take him so that he could use his powers. This Ancient then started moving around the battlefield with Vernon's quickness to deplete others of their life and powers. He was heading towards Vester when Vester slammed a huge boulder down on top of the Ancient. The hills of the battlefield were becoming lifeless boulders while the greenery faded into burnt brown. Ara was dying. Calista shook her head; this couldn't be happening. The Aggies, Jinsons, Karkens and Carpes were doing their best but even their powers were no use against the Ancients who just drained them.

Riso was battling Livinia and Rikar both, neither could let the Ancient touch them so they had to settle for ranged attacks. While most of Livinia's battles consisted of her deadly braids, this one took her evil looking knives. Rikar used his blue flames that barely bothered Riso, who managed to snag one of Livinia's long braids. She let out a shriek as the dark lock started to lose it's color, a whiteness growing up the braid until Rikar cut it with a talon, freeing her from the Ancient who frowned at them. Rikar lifted Livinia in the air and flew them from the Ancient.

Something seemed so familiar, she frowned as she looked around at the battles taking place. Ara was dying, barely any color left, mostly unforgiving terrain. The Ancients were killing Ara with this battle, she could feel Ara weakening beneath her.

"Let's not energize that damn cannon this time." Solen looked over at Kaine who was throwing charged up balls around to push the Ancients back. "Ara will need enough help recovering from this battle without another shot like the last one."

"Hardy har har." Kaine threw Solen a baleful look. "I need to rethink having you as a best friend."

Those words! She had heard them before. Kaine winked at her with a grin while Solen just glared at him. Something wasn't right. An energy blast shot right past her from a Champion whose arm changed into a firing barrel. Eon grabbed the barrel which started to age and deteriorate quickly. She felt as if she was in a fog, unable to breathe as events unfolded around her. She saw the Ancients who had stole powers from the warriors of Ara place their hands on that weapon of theirs. She had hoped that it wouldn't be able to fire after the damage it had done to Ara. But as she watched it was starting to glow just like before.

"C'mon Kaine, where's your sense of adventure?" Solen's amused response had her freezing there. Her dream! No! She looked at him, her eyes filled with dread. "You okay, Spider?" he asked as his smile slipped slightly, his brow furrowing at her. She shook her head, opening her mouth to tell him he needed to run now but she couldn't speak.

Kaine slammed into Solen, knocking him out of the way as a bright bolt of pure white energy flew past them. The boulder where Solen had been standing in front of blew into thousands of dust particles that showered down over them.

"No, we have to stop this!" She tried shouting to them over the noise of the battle.

"I can't always be around to save your ass." Kaine told Solen as he knelt down just like in her dream, glaring at the Ancients who were moving through the battlefield draining anyone they could touch. "These interlopers really need to be evicted." Kaine sent energy coursing along the ground towards the Ancients and their Champions.

"Spider! Watch out!" Appearing next to her from nowhere, Solen grabbed her, twirling them both around and pressing her up against a boulder on the opposite side. The boulder she had been standing in front of exploded to dust. "That was close, Spider. Can't have you getting hurt." He grinned down at her, tilting his head, he kissed her softly. She felt the world tilting around her, slowing down as if her brother, Eon had slowed time. Things felt as if they were moving in slow motion. Solen went to turn back to the battle at hand. She reached for his arm, intending on shimmering them away from there before the nightmare had the time to come true, but it was too late. She saw the flash of light explode from behind him, then the surprised look on his face just as it had happened in her nightmare, had her screaming.

"SOLEN! NOOOO!"

The world went silent around her, all she could hear was the pounding of her heart beating. Solen's eyes were wide open in shock as his body slumped in her arms. They sank to the ground together, Calista holding onto him all the while shaking her head, feeling the rage building within her. "This can't be happening, no this just can't be happening. I just got you back." Her voice broke with the unshed tears that blurred her vision.

Solen, ever so slowly reached up to cup her cheek. With that touch, her tears started to fall as she stared into his eyes that were slowly going dim. His hand moved down from her cheek, down to her chest where the pendant lay that held her beloved Scratch. His hand closed around the pendant as he spoke, his voice low as a whisper. "For you, Spider, my love." His fingers started to glow, then the glow traveled to the pendant. As if the pendant were made of ice, it melted away until Scratch was standing there in Solen's hand.

"Take care of her, little guy." Solen spoke to Scratch who gave a small nod then moved to his favorite perch on her shoulder. "Spider," Solen said, looking into her eyes. "I'm sorry we didn't get our time together. But I'm glad you were here at the end. I love you, Spider. Never forget..." Then, Solen closed his eyes slowly with a smile, his body going still in her arms. Resting her head on Solen's chest, Calista could feel the rage building even more within her. Raising her head towards the sky, not able to control the power emanating from her eyes, she let out a scream that echoed through the battlefield.

"Noooo!"

CHAPTER 23

A life given.
A pain that burns.
A hazy vision.
A life returns.

She had believed the life given was Draken's, believing her dream meant nothing. Solen still lay in her arms, she couldn't let him go. She felt removed from the whole situation, as if she was on the outside looking in. The pain that wracked her body blocked out everything. The sounds of the battle still raging, the images of losses from both sides, none could penetrate the bubble of pain she found herself in. All that mattered was that she had just lost the person that she truly loved, and in such a short time after Draken's death. She still hadn't been able to process Draken's death and now this.

It was too much.

The feeling of Scratch's leg softly caressing her neck brought her back to reality with a crash. Solen's final gift to her, bringing her best friend back. How many times had she wished for Scratch to once again ride on her shoulder? She could feel Scratch's concern for her through their connection. Her eyes were now dry, she didn't think she had it in her to cry anymore.

"Princess?"

She looked up at Rikar staring down at her, the compassion in his eyes almost undoing her. She gave a nod, leaning against his leg. She didn't know if she was nodding in acknowledgement to the title or to try to convey that she was all right. Although, it didn't take a genius to know she wasn't even close to all right. Livinia watched her from Rikar's side, her normally unexpressive face conveyed an unusual concern.

"No, no, nooooo!!" Kaine fell to his knees next to her as he stared at his best friend. "By Ara, NOO!" He screamed.

Eon appeared standing behind her, his hands on her shoulders, giving her a comforting squeeze as she stared down at Solen. Allen rushed to his brother shaking his head, laying his head on his brother's hand, his body shaking as he cried.

A scream had her turning her head to see Lizbet falling to her knees in grief seeing Solen laying there. The numbness that kept her still melted away as a new anger filled her. If not for Lizbet's jealousy both Draken and Solen would still be here. She had no right to mourn. The desire to strike Lizbet down where she stood rode Calista hard.

"Stand up."

Was that Draken's voice? She looked around but saw nothing different and definitely no Draken.

"Petty anger will not win this war." Solen? She looked down at him expecting to see him smiling up at her but all she saw was his lifeless body still in her arms. She looked around her but everyone was still looking at Solen, except for Rikar. He was looking around them as well, did he hear them too?

"Stand up, princess." A more forceful tone from what she thought was Draken's voice. She looked at Rikar who nodded, whether in support or that he too had heard Draken and Solen she didn't know. She looked down at Solen, leaning down she placed a kiss on his forehead and then stood. Scratch moved to settle right in the curve of her neck, letting her know that he wasn't leaving her.

She moved away from Solen and the others, ignoring the ones calling her name. She knew what she had to do. "Calista!" Kaine jumped up to intercept her but Rikar stopped him.

"Leave her be, she knows what she needs to do."

She didn't look back to see if Kaine listened to him or not, she kept walking forward. She had missed out on loving parents while growing up, and Solen had reunited her with them. She met Draken and Rikar who helped her to learn about her true heritage after Solen had left her to battle the Ancients. She left her home to get away from the pain. Kaine came to her so that she and the brothers flew to the stars where she was once again reunited with Solen. In less than a week she lost both Draken and Solen.

She rode that pain as she walked, let it fill her until it flowed from her in a hazy vision of yellow, red and blue that surrounded her. She didn't even realize the ones who were moving out of her way, staring at her in awe. Later she would be told that they could barely see her within the phoenix that moved with her. As she moved, they saw a mighty blue dragon joining the phoenix, flying around her as she walked. As both images were mere extensions of her. Maybe they were. On her chest the Hunter's symbol glowed brightly.

Her blond hair looked like flames flowing behind her. Her whole body looked as if she was walking through flames, although she knew none of this. She moved forward in her anger, pain and torment.

"You got this!"

"Show them who you are, princess!"

"Let's end this!"

She didn't know if it was only in her head, hearing Solen's and Draken's voices, but she didn't care. It was comforting to her, it helped her move. Then a feminine voice spoke up.

"All of Ara, past and present walk with you. You are not alone."

She didn't know that voice, and wondered if it was Ara. She sent a silent apology to her for not being able to protect her.

"No death is in vain, for every life that is saved, you will come closer to ending the reign of the Ancients."

She barely contained a snort, she felt as if she had failed. No life is more important than any others. She didn't want to lose anyone. A light rub of Scratch's leg on her neck had her absently moving to pet him, to reassure him.

"You must find the source of the Ancient's powers to completely defeat them. You must defeat their queen, without her, they are nothing."

Calista nodded, turning to watch the Ancients ordering their Champions to stop her. They tried. They lunged at her but as soon as they entered the light around her they would disintegrate. She kept moving forward as they now ran from her. It mattered not, she knew none of them would leave Ara alive. She raised her arm as volleys of energy arrows shot out, disintegrating all they hit, including the ships that were attempting to take off. All that was left on Ara was the ship with the cannon, where Risa, Riso and Ryno stood, screaming at the Champions to get them out of there. She lifted both her arms and let the dragon and phoenix loose on the ship, it exploded into dust particles.

No more ships, Ancients or Champions were left on Ara but she wasn't done. She looked up to see ships attempting to leave. Raising a hand she once again sent the dragon and phoenix forward, with the destruction of each ship, a bright light would glow in the sky. When there was nothing left, when all their enemies had been vanquished, only then did she fall to her knees letting all the anger and pain out in one long loud scream that created shockwaves all around her.

She could feel the pain all around as others mourned their losses as well. Vester howled over Vernon's body as their sister wept. The Aggies and their cousins were gathered around Sander's body as well as some others. The colors of Ara had diminished, only an empty shell of a world remained. She closed her eyes as darkness claimed her.

Scratch was the first thing she saw when she opened her eyes. He was sitting on her chest staring at her, when he saw her eyes open, he rose and she could feel his happiness at his mistress being awake. She pulled herself up as Scratch moved to her shoulder, moving to sit on the bed. She was in the room that Solen's parents had been letting her use and Brooke was sitting in the chair by the window. She looked around the room, the potted plants were dead and brown.

"You're awake." She looked over at Brooke who was watching her with a relieved expression. Brooke nodded to Scratch. "He wouldn't let anyone remove him, he stayed there on your chest for the past several days."

"Several?" Did she hear right?

Brooke nodded. "You've been out for several days;

we were all beginning to worry that you wouldn't wake up."

Calista stood up on shaky legs, Brooke moved quickly to help her. "Thank you." Calista attempted to smile at her but it felt unnatural. Her whole being was numb. They moved through the empty house, the vibrant colors from before had faded. Moving outside she had another shock, besides all the dead foliage around the village, the fire of Ara was nothing more than an empty pit in the middle of town.

"Yes, the fire of Ara has gone out." She turned her head to see Grint walking up to them. "Ara is dying."

"Where is everyone?" She looked around but saw no one in the village.

"Preparing our fallen for funeral, although without the fire of Ara, it won't be the one they deserve." She could hear the sadness in his voice.

"There will be a fire," she told him.

"How?" he asked her.

"I will light the fire for Ara, one last time." She didn't know how she knew, but she knew she could do it.

Grint nodded in reverence. "That would be greatly appreciated, I will tell everyone to come here."

"No." He frowned at her words. "It will be done in the pool at Sala Way."

Grint smiled at her, giving a slight bow. "Much more appropriate, I see you are connected with Ara. She has chosen well."

Connected with Ara? Is that why she knew she could do it and where it should be done? Was Ara the feminine voice she had heard? She would speak with Grint about it but not now. She nodded to him and watched as he moved away to spread the news.

Brooke looked up at her. "I'm glad Solen and the others are getting the funeral they deserve. Thank you." Calista nodded; she didn't trust her own voice right now. "I'll help you get ready for the funeral."

Once again, all four factions were gathered in Sala Way, although this wasn't a time of celebration as it was before. The pool in the center that had contained the water was nothing more than a hole within the ground that they could see no bottom. There were no glaciers, water falls, rivers of lava, trees or bushes. It looked as desolate as the deserts back home. So many bodies wrapped in silken refinery that lay on marble gurneys.

Grint stood up, no need to ask for silence, no one knew what to say anyways. "Tonight, we put to rest our loved ones who gave their lives in the battle against evil. The fires of Ara will burn one last time and take these warriors home with her." He looked to Calista who moved forward, walking into the empty hole until she stood in the center. There was no ground beneath her feet but she didn't need ground to stand where she was. She closed her eyes feeling the fires burning within her, opening her eyes she released those fires, creating the fire of Ara. Scratch was sitting on Brooke's shoulder outside the pool, his eyes never leaving Calista.

"Rest thy warrior within Ara's embrace.

Within Ara you will find your place.

Your battles have been fought; your wars are done.

Rest within Ara as one of her daughters, and one of her sons."

Everyone started to sing the song that Calista had heard at Draken's funeral as they moved forward with the gurneys. She stood there watching as the Floe nation placed their people on the edge of the pool. She would pull them in with her, watching as the flames caressed the bodies until there was nothing, not even the marble gurneys. With each one she watched as the person's corporeal shell disintegrated, leaving a sentient incorporeal vision of the person standing there. Each one turned to see her there, nodded and mouthed thank you before they sank below the fires into Ara.

She hadn't known that would happen; she hadn't been prepared. For each nation it was the same. The Pyre nation and the Pura nation. The Aggies, the Karkens, the Jinsons and the Carpes. Each one turned to nod and give their thanks. Now it was time for the ones from Solen's nation. She couldn't do this; she couldn't say goodbye to him again. Each one nodded and thanked her as tears coursed down her cheeks, she knew what was coming. When Vernon rose, he smiled at her, sympathy shining in his eyes as he knew what she would have to face. He nodded, winked and mouthed thank you before descending into the fire.

The last gurney was being placed on the edge of the pool, she knew who was wrapped in the silken refinery that had spiders etched all through it. She didn't want to be the one to pull him into the fire but if she didn't he wouldn't be with Ara, something that she knew she couldn't let happen. No matter how hard it was for her. She pulled Solen into the fire, watched as the fire shred his corporeal body. When he rose and saw her, he smiled at her. His incorporeal body floated towards her, she didn't know how he was doing this but she reached for him. Her hand moved through him, making it more real.

"Spider, you've given my people a most generous gift." He told her.

She shook her head. "Don't leave me Solen, not again."

"I wish I could give you what you want, I'm sorry that I'm leaving you but I won't apologize for giving my life to save yours. I would do it all over again if I had to."

"I never wanted you to." She protested.

His hand moved to her chest, placed over her heart although she could feel nothing. "I'll always be here." He looked to where Scratch was sitting on Brooke's shoulder. "A part of me will always be with your best friend as well." He looked back at her. "A gift that I could only give to my true partner, with Ara's blessing."

"I want to go with you." She cried.

He shook his head. "You can't Spider and you know that."

"Why not?"

"Ara told you what you have to do, you need to find the source of the Ancient's powers. Their queen. Find her and destroy her. Only then will the universe be safe."

"Then we can be together?" She knew what she was asking, she knew it was wrong but she didn't care. She just wanted to be with him.

He shook his head. "I will be here waiting for you when your time comes but until then, promise me you will live, Spider. Promise me." He stared at her as the fires started to dim. "I won't go into Ara until you promise me, the fire dies out and I will never be able to be with Ara. Promise me, Spider."

"I promise." She choked out, she felt the ghost kiss he gave her before he nodded and descended into Ara while she cried, the fires dying around her. It was Rikar who swooped in to catch her before she fell into the hole and laid her gently on the ground by the pool. She couldn't look at anyone as she just stared into space, she had taken all she could.

CHAPTER 24

Calista walked out of the village towards the ship where she would be leaving with the others. Her hair was pulled back in a pony tail that hung down past the hem of her black half shirt. Blue suspenders attached to the back of her black jeans, crisscrossing over her chest and attaching to the waist. On her shoulder sat Scratch, in his favorite position once again. As she walked forward the sound of her boots on the hardened ground below worked with the rhythm of her heart. There standing outside the ship with Grint were those who would be going on this journey with her. Rikar, Livinia, Eon, Kaine, Allen and Vester stood there while Stryx, Clyde and Claire were getting the ship ready for takeoff.

They were chatting with Grint who was wearing casual clothing, gone was the armor. He turned, smiling when he saw her coming. She wished she could return the smile but she had nothing in her to give, so she just nodded in greeting.

"So, you're leaving." It wasn't a question so she didn't bother to answer. "Where will you be going?"

"To find the Ancient's queen."

"Do you know where to start?" Grint asked her.

"No." She had to admit but she told him about the feminine voice that spoke to her and what it said.

He nodded at her. "It was as I thought, Ara had spoken with you. She has taken you in as one of her children."

She wasn't sure what to say so she stayed silent.

"Once a child of Ara, always a child of Ara." He told her, holding out a necklace to her with a shiny pendant hanging from the chain. "This is a piece of Ara, no matter where you go, a part of Ara will always be with you." She looked at the pendant and could see the different layers of Ara. Green for the realm of the Aggies, white for the realm of the Jinsons, red for the realm of the Karkens and blue at the very bottom for the realm of the Carpes.

"Thank you." She looked up at him from the pendant, placing it around her neck. Seemed she traded one pendant for another.

"You're welcome. Maybe it could be some help in guiding you along the way."

"Do you know where their queen is?" She asked him, unfortunately he shook his head.

"That is one mystery that very few know, the Ancients keep that knowledge very well hidden." He grimaced. "I wish I could be of more help."

She nodded, looking around seeing others walking with boxes and bags. "Where is everyone going?"

"We have several ships that is equipped for the different factions of Ara, we will be leaving to find a new home while Ara heals herself. The Aggies and their cousins will be staying with Ara to help her heal." He breathed in shakily. "And Lizbet will be staying as well."

"Lizbet?" Calista tilted her head.

Grint nodded. "She has chosen of her own free will to stay with Ara as penance for her crimes. She will work with the Aggies and their cousins with my blessing." His words were tightly spoken, she couldn't imagine the feelings he was dealing with right now. "I must be going now, time for us to leave Ara and find a new home. I hope that one day our paths will cross again in our travels." Placing his arms around her and giving her a hug he told her, "safe travels, child of Ara." Then, he nodded his head before he turned to leave.

Calista watched him as he left, watched Kaine's and Brooke's tearful goodbyes, looked around Ara at the desolation that was left. The Ancients and their queen had a lot to answer for. She would be their judge, jury and executioner.

She stood on the bridge of the ship, leaning on the railing that went around the walkway in the back. Stryx was at his console while Clyde and Claire were at theirs, guiding the ship from Ara into the stars. No one knew their destination, just that they needed to find the Ancients and their queen.

"Calista." She turned to see her brother staring at her back. "Your tattoo."

She looked down at her side and frowned. "It's gone." Sure enough, the phoenix tattoo that had adorned her side for so long was no longer there.

"Your back." He pointed to her back.

She turned and moved her shirt to see the reflection in the metal panel. There on her back was her phoenix with a mighty blue dragon, in the top center was the hunter's symbol. She readjusted herself and sighed, so she would always have Draken and Solen with her. She wished that it made her feel better but right now there was only one thing that would ease the pain within her.

"So, what now?" Stryx looked at her.

Staring emotionless at the view screen into the abyss in front of them, in a very cold voice, all Calista could say was. "Vengeance."

A Note from the Author

When I first wrote Spider's Awakening, I hadn't planned on it being more than one book. I had created Calista as a personal challenge to myself, because of my own fear of spiders. Then along came the two dragon brothers who were inspired by two wonderful friends, I enjoyed watching the brothers come to life between the pages of my story. I had such fun but I never planned for it to go any further.

There were some who had commented that they had hoped there would be more, I had been informed by them that I couldn't stop the story there. None were more louder than a certain someone who kept throwing ideas at me for a second book, until one of those ideas stuck with me. He would brainstorm with me during long drives and together we came up with the Spider's Triad series.

This book is a collaboration of our ideas that will extend into the final book of the series, Spider's Vengeance. This three-book series is brought to you with the help of Paul Bush who is the co-author and the reason for it all.

All I can say is blame Paul.

REVELATION 20: 7-15

But fire came down from heaven and devoured them. And the devil, who deceived them, was thrown into the lake of burning sulfur, where the beast and the false prophet had been thrown.

They will be tormented day and night for ever and ever. Then I saw a great white throne and him who was seated on it.

About the Author

TL Shively is an award-winning author who loves her husband and three boys; they are not only a lot of her inspiration but also her greatest supporters. She is very outnumbered in a house full of boys; even their dog is male.

Her whole life has been full of stories that used to be only in her head, entertaining her when she was younger and lived in the country where the nearest neighbor was miles down the road. It wasn't until she was much older that she finally put these stories down on paper, and it was the Sanctuary Guardian's story that came out.

She loves anything fantasy: gaming, reading, writing, knick-knacks, you name it. She loves crafting of almost any kind and comes from a very artistic family.

OTHER BOOKS BY THE AUTHOR

SANCTUARY GUARDIAN SERIES READING ORDER:
The Secret Sanctuary
The Town That Time Forgot
The Battle of Sleeping Lady
The Independence Mine Disaster
The Hunter's Betrayal
Haven's Shadow
A Sanctuary Christmas

SPIDER'S TRILOGY
Spider's Awakening
Spider's Return

ALSO FROM AUTHOR:
Sanctuary and Friends coloring book

www.ingramcontent.com/pod-product-compliance
Lightning Source LLC
Chambersburg PA
CBHW030110260626
47156CB00008B/2604